I0708433

Also by Rose Hammond

Idlewild & Woodland Park, MI
(An African American Remembers)

Just a Poor Country Girl

Transitions

The Documentary
In Between the Trees (An African American Remembers) Idlewild
& Woodland Park, MI

INTRODUCTION

Our family uprooted from Mississippi to a northern, rural town called Baldwin, Michigan. At a church fellowship meeting, Grandma met a lady who sold her nearly 40 acres of land 35 miles south in another rural town called White Cloud.

At that time, African Americans were not able to live inside the "city limits" so our families built houses next to each other seven miles outside, the "city limits", just as they had lived in Natchez, Mississippi. Although there were very few African Americans who lived in the area, our families taught us how to survive. Our home was built in between aunts, uncles, and grandparents. It was a quaint two-bedroom house with a leaky roof, not large enough for the eight of us. But we managed.

Under the Weeping Willow Tree is the continuation story, Part 2 of the book Transitions that is loosely based on young Maggie Dorsey's (aka Rose L. Hammond), coming of life journey as she enters junior high school. Maggie is part of a siblingship of four brothers and one sister, but a divided home. The family's livelihood is the welfare system and picking crops.

Many nights she'd pray for her father's return saying, "Oh God, please hear my prayer and bring our daddy back home. I don't want to put my hands into the dark muck dirt, topping no man's onions or picking any damn cherries anymore. Sorry God, I mean no cherries."

There are a few bright spots in her life, her three best friends who do most things together except pick crops and when the aunts, uncles, grandparents and her family eat lunch and dinner underneath the weeping willow tree.

Under the Weeping Willow Tree begins with Chapter 20 where the book Transitions ends with Chapter 19.

Note

· · · ·

A Happy Home Recipe
(Written the way Charley Louise Hammond wrote her recipes)

4c's of love   *2 spoons of tenderness*
2c's of loyalty   *4 qtrs of faith*
1c of friendship   *1 barrel of laughter*
5 spoons of hope

Take love and loyalty, mix it thoroughly with faith. Blend it with tenderness. Add friendship and hope, sprinkle abundantly with laughter, bake it with sunshine. Serve daily with generous helping of forgiveness. In a lifetime everyone faces challenges. But without those challenges you will not experience growth.

Charley Louise Hammond (mama)

Recipe as written by Charley Louise Hammond. Permission given.

Under The Weeping Willow Tree

"A coming of age story"

Chapter 20

(Chapter continuation from the book entitled "Transitions")
Maggie's last name will be updated to the family name of Hammond

The Fields

Travel north on M-37, past Newaygo, and you will arrive in the small town of White Cloud, the Newaygo County seat. As you drive toward the town, you will not miss a taller-than-life sign that reads "Where the north begins and the pure waters flow." That sign seems to be held in the highest regard because it is high enough for anyone and everyone to read. I don't know who came up with the slogan, but if you didn't remember anything else about White Cloud, you remembered that sign.

. . . .

When I grew up in White Cloud, there were the usual amenities similar to the larger cities near us, such as Saginaw, Flint, and Grand Rapids, but on a much smaller scale. I remember Mama going to Grand Rapids for the bulk of our groceries that we didn't grow and shopping for our school clothes that she didn't sew herself.

We lived on a gravel road, on Rural Route 1. Most Sundays, I'd stare out the car window as the family drove, one car behind the other, to the White Cloud Church of God In Christ, located about six miles outside the city limits. My two uncles worked in town, one at a factory and the other as a janitor at the court house.

The majority of the time, Blacks and Caucasians were together at schools, sports events, and town events, such as parades and carnivals. My two older brothers and I were close in age and attended White Cloud Elementary School together until they moved down the hill to the high school building, which included junior high. One brother,Thomas, and I remained at the elementary school.

• • • •

I didn't know which was louder: the rain hitting the roof or the rain splattering inside the largest bucket that Edward, my brother, could find to put in the living room. A bucket was placed in the living room whenever it rained to catch drops from the leaky roof. Edward didn't want to get up and check it throughout the night, so he grabbed the largest bucket.

"Oh shoot." I shoved the covers from around me and walked quickly to the window. I pulled the curtains aside slowly, not wanting to see anything that resembled rain. There it was, coming down as if to laugh at me, having a joyous time splattering everywhere. If the rain didn't stop by recess, my class would have to stay inside, and the leaf house we made in the woods near school would be ruined.

There was nothing that could be done now except get dressed and pray for the rain to stop. I tried to remember important facts about our town for history class: Who is the mayor? Where is the county seat? Stuff like that.

My brother, Mike, yelled for me to hurry because the bus was on its way. I looked at the clock. He was right. Our bus had a flat nose in the front. Each morning I'd see the bus pass by our house, going toward Robinson Lake to pick up those kids first, which always bothered us. Why drive away from our house only to have to come back and pick the rest of us up, along with the Hammonds, McKinneys, Glovers, and Garrisons?

Usually, one of my brothers or I would stand inside the front porch to see when the bus was coming. This morning we woke up late. The driver honked, expecting four families to run out of their houses. Whenever it rained, the other families either squeezed inside our front porch or stayed inside their own houses, peeking out their windows. If everyone wasn't there, someone would try to stall the driver. We'd walk slower, talk to the driver about nothing much, or try something else. Usually, the driver caught on to our tactics and slowly drove off, looking in the side mirror. My brothers knew that if the Hammonds missed the bus, they'd better get to school somehow and not let Mama find out.

I yelled from the back of the bus, "Wait! Here comes my brother!"

Mr. Hucklebee, the driver, slammed on the brakes. "You got lucky this time, Mike. Next time you'd better get up earlier."

We hardly had time to swallow our breakfast. I don't remember much chewing. The dishes were left in the kitchen sink, which was a big no-no. Mama had already gone to work, and, someone would have to have to explain why the dishes were left.

The bus driver pulled away from our house as if he was in a hurry, causing Mike to walk past my seat in a jerking motion. If he hadn't gripped onto the seat next to him, he would have surely fallen. In passing, he whispered to me, "Don't worry." With Daddy gone, Mike stepped into, somewhat, Daddy's role, meaning he was the one who usually explained to Mama about any unfinished chore.

I let out a sigh of relief because this morning had been my turn to wash the dishes. I sat back against my seat and began to think about the leaf house my friends and I made. Each of us had one room.

My friends are Cheryl, Jackie, Sarah. We played together at recess. The elementary school had a new addition: a fifth and sixth grade entrance with its own hallway. The fifth grade class no longer had to share the playground with the other elementary kids (we called them "little ones").

Since the fifth graders had moved to another side of the school, we had to find a new area between the trees to make our new house. We brushed leaves together with the broken tree branches. Cheryl remade the kitchen because she liked to cook and Jackie, the two bedrooms, Sarah, the dining room and me, the living room. Together we made the front porch and doorway. The branches that had fallen from the trees formed the outside of the house. After we ate lunch, the first thing we did was run to the new house.

Thank goodness by the time we got to school the rain had

stopped. We noticed some of the leaves of our leaf house clumped together from the rain, but we spread them around. Then I froze, staring in one direction.

"Maggie, what's wrong with you?" Cheryl asked.

With eyes squinted and lips tightened, I pointed.

Cheryl's shoulders slumped. "Oh no. Why do you let that girl and her stupid friends bother you?"

"Because they think they're sooo popular and better than anyone," I said.

My friends surrounded me. I kicked the leaves in frustration. "That doesn't give Susan and her friends -"

"Stop it," Cheryl said. "They are sooo popular, the most popular girls in the fifth grade, and none of them like us coloreds, saying 'nigger' in whispers when they walk past us, thinking we can't hear them. So, keep your wits. You don't want your mama comin' up here."

The bell rang for us to get in line and go inside the school. One of us would usually linger to make sure Susan's group didn't mess up our house, staying until our teacher told us to get in line with the rest of the class. Today was my turn to linger until Miss Carol yelled out my name.

When we went back to class after lunch, Miss Carol stood in front of us holding white envelopes in her hand. With an unusual tone, one that was almost sad, she said, "What I have in my hand is a very important letter. Please give it to your parents immediately when you get home."

Everyone began looking around at each other, whispering and wondering. Was she leaving? Were our parents given the name of a new teacher for the sixth grade? The commotion inside the classroom grew louder and louder.

"Class. PLEASE BE QUIET."

All at once, there was silence.

"The letter reads: 'This letter is to inform all parents who have students in the fifth grade that will be moving on to the sixth grade that effective the upcoming school year, your child's class will be moving to the White Cloud Junior High School wing of the White Cloud High School building. Everyone will be welcomed the first day of the next school year. If you have any questions, please contact the White Cloud High School office. The telephone number is listed at the bottom of this letter. Sincerely, your principal.'"

Miss Carol reminded us in a stern voice to give the letter to our parents as soon as we got home. She sat down at her desk with her hands folded. "Class, I will sincerely miss each and every one of you. I know you will do well down the hill. When you leave today, I will hand your letter to you."

I sat thinking. *Tomorrow will be the end of our school year. It went by fast. Everything is about to change. Here I thought there would be another year for us to enjoy ourselves and to prepare for those junior high girls down the hill.*

Cheryl, who sat across from me, had lowered her head. She fumbled with her fingers. Without looking toward me, she spoke in a sad voice. "I'm not ready to go down the hill. That's the darn high school."

"Me either," I responded.

"But, you have older brothers. Family. I don't have anyone there. Every time we've gone to the football or basketball games, the upper-class girls treated us as if they were better, telling us to go and sit in our area. Now we'll see them everyday."

I stood up, put my hands on my hips, and stomped my foot. "I'm not ready to go down that hill. We'll have to stick together because, no matter what, the sixth grade will be part of the junior high and high school."

After I gave my surprise follow-your-leader speech, no one said a word, everyone's eyes stationary on me, until a girl blurted out, "I guess the class has just found the president for the sixth grade." The entire class stared at me again, some with eyes wide open.

I couldn't believe what I had just said or done. I was usually the quietest one in the room. I looked at Miss Carol. Even she looked surprised.

"Miss Hammond, where did that come from?" Miss Carol asked.

"I, I don't know. It just came out."

When I sat down, the class clapped.

Someone said, "Madam President?"

"No." I stuttered. "No."

Two of the popular girls were in my class. Our eyes met. "We'll see you down the hill, so-called Madam President."

· · · ·

That brings me to the end of this school day, the last day of school with the infamous letter tightly clinched in my hand. The school bus driver closed the door and began to drive away. I was slumped in my seat, but my attitude had changed to happiness.

Shirley, the person I usually shared my seat, with wasn't here. This gave me the opportunity to move from the window seat to the aisle and not be squeezed against the window.

The bus was two houses away from my home when I turned around toward the back to see what my brothers were doing. Mike and Edward were laughing with the Harris brothers, who lived two houses from ours but got off the bus with us.

During the school year, a rule in our house, and there were many, was to change from our school clothes into our everyday clothes of pants, t-shirt, or blouse before running outside to play or talking to Mama with any school concerns. But today I wanted to talk to Mama first. When Mr. Hucklebee stopped the bus, I lunged out of my seat.

"Stop that running!" Mr. Hucklebee yelled.

I slowed down to a fast walk. When the bus door opened, Mike, Edward, and Thomas were in the middle of the bus. I stumbled on the bottom step and fell onto the gravel driveway. My brothers laughed and ran past me. But, instead of chasing them to the back door of the house, I ran to the front door of the porch where we watched for the bus in the mornings, which was a shorter distance. By the time my brothers noticed I wasn't behind them, it was too late.

Running into the house, I yelled, "Mama!"

"What's all that commotion?" she asked.

I had the letter in my hand and ran toward her voice. Our house wasn't very large, and you could tell which part of the house the voice came from by listening, which my brothers didn't do too well. Mama's voice came from the kitchen. The living room and kitchen were visible through the large square opening in the middle of the wall between them. The living room was the first room you entered coming from the front porch. I pushed the door open, leaped onto the couch, reached my hand through the opening into the kitchen, and hollered, "Mama! Mama!" She took my letter first.

"I'm trying to prepare dinner. What's all the fuss? And how many times have I told you kids to come into the house and change from your school clothes into your every day clothes before any talk about school? And, Maggie, why are you standing on top the couch?"

I thought, *How on earth can she say so much without taking a breath?* No matter, that was a rule that Mama was firm on because usually the boys would tussle or something before changing and either rip their clothes or somehow get dirty. To some, Mama would come as firm, but she was loving, raising six kids.

Out of breath, in a soft voice, I said, "Mama, I have a very important letter from Miss Carol, my teacher. She told me to give it to you as soon as I got home."

Mama turned down the burner underneath the food cooking on the stove and wiped her hands on her apron. "I hope this letter is very important for you to run through the house like you just did, trying to beat the others to talk to me. And for you, Maggie, to jump onto the couch. I'll read it, but all of you go and change from your school clothes."

The boys' bedroom was off the kitchen. I slept in the bedroom off the living room in the front of the house with my sister and Mama. As I walked to the bedroom to change my clothes, I turned around and noticed Mama walk to the dining table to sit down. Once I got to the bedroom, which was only a few steps away, I pulled the curtains aside and leaned toward the door frame of the bedroom. I wondered if the envelope being ripped open was mine or my brothers'.

Mama must have had a sixth sense or something because

the next words I heard were, "Boys, stop peeking around the corner. Maggie, you too." I waited for her reaction to the letter but nothing happened until a few minutes later when she walked into the living room. "Maggie, come join me in the living room."

I pulled the curtain aside and walked slowly. I sat in the chair next to the piano outside our bedroom. Mama patted her hand on the couch, wanting me to sit next to her. I walked to the couch and plopped down.

"First of all, why are you plopping down on this couch? Let's try it again."

I got up, walked back to the over-sized chair, and back to the couch.

"That's better. Well, it seems as if you'll be in the same building with your older brothers."

I leaned back against the couch. "Yeah," I mumbled.

"You seem to have a strong reaction to that. Can you tell me why?"

I signed. "Mama, it's not that I'll be with Mike and Edward, but . . . before we left school today, I gave a 'we will not be intimidated by the older girls speech.'" I looked toward the floor and back to Mama. "I'm not even a teenager yet. It's too early. I was expecting to stay in the elementary building."

As usual, when Mama would comfort us, she put her arms around my shoulders, giving me a big, cuddly hug. "You'll do just fine", she said. "You're too stubborn to let anyone walk over you."

After our talk, Mama asked me to set the dinner table. We were eating earlier tonight because the elders of the family were going to have a meeting.

Dinner was quieter than usual. I think we all knew what the elders were going to talk about: which field we'd be sweating in this summer, and whether we would be topping onions or picking cherries or string beans.

I folded my arms and looked at Mama. "I have something to say."

"Now young lady," Mama said, "your facial expression looks concerned. Please use your words carefully."

"It's just ... Mama, for once I wish we could have fun like the white kids. Can't you and Daddy get back together?"

Mama just looked at me. My brothers did too. I didn't know if I was gonna get a whippin' or what. Mama asked me to bring my plate to the kitchen. She was about five feet five tall and plump. She walked behind me to the sink. I stood frozen in place, still gripping my plate and silverware. Mama made eye contact with me, but, I wasn't sure what was on her mind or what she was going to say.

"Young lady, face me."

Mama reached to hold onto my chin. Her eyes were filled with tears and her voice was soft. "I don't like that your daddy and I separated either, but I'm doing the best I can to keep food on the table and clothes on you kids' back. Cleaning houses, working the fields, and the little work that I get at the Fremont facility is all we have. Do you understand me?"

With a somber voice, I said, "Yes." I slid my plate and silverware into the soapy water in the sink.

Mama asked me to finish cleaning the dining room table with my brothers.

My brother leaned close to my ear. "You better watch that mouth of yours. That smartness won't work when you get down the hill."

"We won't always be there to protect you," Mike said.

I brushed them away.

A few hours later, Mama returned from the family meeting

and called all of us into the living room. She sat in the oversized, dilapidated chair. Mike and Edward sat on the piano stool while the rest of us sat on the sofa. She twiddled her fingers and said, "Starting in a week, the family will pick cherries." She paused. I crossed my fingers, praying silently, *Please, please, God, no onions.* Mama looked into each of our eyes. "And topping onions into the school year." My shoulders slumped. My body fell limp against the sofa.

I thought to myself, *For one damn summer, could we not have to top onions? Is this all that's left, and welfare?*

Mama told us to follow her into the dining room. "All of our earnings will be put inside this china cabinet." There were designated glasses for each of us kids, including the twins, who would share a glass. All the money would be used to buy school clothing and supplies.

• • • •

Today is a half day of school and very hot. I wore my pink paddle pushers, the ones with the wide stripes - my favorites - with a short sleeve blouse. While sitting at my desk, I folded my arms, rested my chin on them, and listened to the kids chatter.

Some talked about their summer plans. This was our last day of elementary school.

I began to think about Daddy. I wondered why we couldn't spend part of the summer with him in Chicago.

The bell rang. Kids scrambled out of their desks and rushed to the door.

Miss Carol hollered, "Stop running!" Some did, but most squeezed through the door, bumping into each other, like someone was handing out dollar bills in the hallway.

I turned around and waved. Miss Carol waved back reminding everyone to walk and to have a good summer.

Sarah and Jackie sat on the school steps while Cheryl and I stood holding onto our notebooks.

"Sarah, what are you doin' this summer?" I asked.

"My father is gonna stay here and work while the rest of us visit cousins down South. We'll be back near the middle of summer." Sarah rubbed one foot against the bottom step.

Jackie watched ants run in and out of an ant hill. She found a stick on the ground next to her and rubbed it across the ant hill. Ants scattered. She told us that she didn't know what she was doing this summer, that her family hadn't made up their minds.

"Cheryl, what about you?" Jackie asked.

"Well . . . I'm not sure." Cheryl frowned and seemed less than excited.

"What's wrong? You don't look happy," I said.

"Never mind," Cheryl frowned.

"What about you Maggie?"

I wondered if I should make something up or just tell the truth. *Why can't I say something exciting, like we're goin' on a long summer vacation?* Instead, I told the truth, partly. "My family doesn't have any plans for the summer."

Jackie looked surprised. "You won't have to pick crops?"

The bus drivers honked their horns, warning they would leave soon.

I sighed. What a relief. I waved to my friends and walked to the bus.

Mr. Hucklebee said, "You better get on this bus before you get left, Ms. Hammond, and have to catch a ride with your uncle at the court house."

I hurried to my usual seat and pulled the window down to see if any of my friends had gotten on their buses.

Then I heard an annoying voice. "Ms. Hammond," Mr.

Hucklebee said, "you know you're not supposed to open the window unless you ask." My first reaction was to slam the window shut, but after hearing Mama's voice of reason inside my head, I merely closed the window.

. . . .

It was five-thirty on a Monday morning. I dreamt I was sitting on the beach with my friends, pushing the sand in between my toes. I felt someone's hand push against my body. Then a voice said, "Rise and shine. Give God the glory."

My eyes cracked open. There was Mama. As I leaned against the headboard, I immediately noticed that this was not a beach.

No matter what the occasion, Mama said the same thing: Rise and shine. Give God the glory. Those cherries aren't gonna pick themselves, young lady."

I wanted to slump back underneath the covers and go back to my dream. *Where did she get that saying from? I wondered.* Somehow, in the summer, it eased the pain of getting up at five-thirty in the morning Monday through Friday and sometimes on Saturday.

I walked to the window, prayed for rain, and slowly pulled the curtains aside. There was no rain. Just a little bit of fog.

Mary sleepwalked to the bathroom, meaning her eyes were half closed. I grabbed her before she fell.

This would be the first time that she and her twin, Joe, would pick cherries. They had gone to the fields before but never picked cherries.

As Mary and I stumbled to the bathroom, Mama said from the kitchen, "Remember to dress Mary in warm clothes, Maggie!"

Oh God, what will this day be like? I thought to myself.

My brothers and Mary and I wore hooded sweatshirts with short-sleeve shirts underneath. Close to noon, when the weather warmed up, we'd layer down. That's what all croppers - what we called ourselves - did.

Mike and Edward packed the coolers with water, Kool-Aid, snacks, and lunches. Mike came back into the house and told Mama that Aunt Louise and James, her adopted son, were waiting in their car parked in the driveway.

"Hurry up, kids, before Aunt Louise honks her horn."

Mike hurried to get Joe and helped him put on his hat, sweatshirt and coat. Edward was at the dining room table, tying his shoes. He took his darn good ole time. Mama encouraged all of us to hurry. Mary didn't seem to be in a hurry, so I walked her out the door.

Mama asked Edward again to hurry up. "No matter how slow you tie those shoe, you are still gonna pick cherries."

Not long after leaving, the twins fell asleep. *This would be the perfect time to talk to Mama about the twins' first time picking cherries,* I thought. They would have to learn to pick without eating them, at a quick pace. After all, I began picking around the same age - six years old.

"Mama?" I spoke to her with my head down, twiddling my fingers. "What do you think about the twins being croppers?"

Mama was a careful driver, especially this time of the morning, because the roads were two-track. She didn't take her eyes off the road and said quietly, "I don't know. Just keep an eye on Mary, okay?" Mary sat in between us. I pulled her closer to me.

Mike and Edward were responsible for Joe, Mary's twin. All six of us Hammonds worked the fields to make extra money. I loved my dad but hated our circumstances, not understanding why he didn't help. At least, not that I knew. The grownups didn't talk business around us kids, believing that we were told what we needed to know.

I leaned my head against the window, thinking that maybe this is why the family decided to pick cherries instead of onions. Cherries were easier. There was shade from the trees and the twins could rest next to us underneath the trees. In the onion fields, the sun beat against your body, and the black muck dirt smell lingered underneath your fingernails and in your clothes. Kids teased us, calling us "onion kids." They could smell the stench of those onions.

I fell asleep until my head bumped against the window and I heard our car's squeaky brakes. I rubbed my eyes. Most of the fog had disappeared. The road to the orchards were no different than the onion fields, except some were bumpier. The thick tree branches leaned so far that they almost reached each other across the two track.

Mama drove slowly, searching for the perfect spot to park. Aunt Louise parked behind us. Other cars were already there. I noticed a tall, thin man with a bushy beard. He was almost as tall as Uncle Ted. He stood in front of three other families and pointed in the opposite direction of our cars.

Mama and Aunt Louise walked toward the man. He turned

around and stopped his conversation, took off his cap, and rubbed the top of his head. Then he waved and yelled, "Good morning."

Mama waved back. She pointed toward our cars.

Snickering to myself, I thought, *Why does he have the same bald spot as Uncle Ted and rubs or scratches it whenever he takes off his cap? I'm sure it can't itch every time someone talks to him, can it?* I was probably letting my thoughts get the best of me.

The other cars weren't far from ours, the windows were cracked open. Kids laughed inside. As more daylight came across the orchard, I rolled the window down more and smiled at one of the girls.

The man directed Mama in a different direction. Mama must have not understood because he stopped us and hollered, "Ma'am, just follow me." He drove around our cars.

Mama and Aunt Louise parked behind him. Then Mama told us to get out of the car. The grass was tall and wet. The row of cherry trees seemed to reach as far as my eyes could see. When the man got out of his truck, Mama said to us, "This is Mr. Henry, the orchard boss."

We stood side-by-side against the car. Mr. Henry looked at the twins and then at the rest of us. "Good morning," he said.

Mama asked Mike and Edward to carry the cooler with the snacks for our break. Thomas carried the blankets while also trying to hold the twins' hands. We always brought blankets to the fields. Most of the time, the ground was damp.

"Step high," I told Mary.

"Like this?" she asked.

"Look. Watch me and step as high as you can." As I held her hands and tried to carry our blankets, I told her that she was doing good. But honestly, between the tall grass and cherry tree branches, Mary was very clumsy. She'd lift one leg and then the other, as if marching, and brush a cherry tree branch away at the same time.

The cars were parked four or five cherry trees ahead. Our family followed the same routine so that by the time we would have our break, we'd move the cars up four or five more trees. This was a way for Mama and Aunt Louise to keep track of our buckets and money. Mama figured that by this time, the twins were tired, and she'd let them lie inside the car to rest. We could keep an eye on them.

"The weeds are too high," Joe complained. He didn't move from where he was standing.

Throughout the day, we'd encourage the twins to stomp

down on the weeds like they were killing ants in our backyard, and to keep walking around the tree to the next branch. They both looked at me and laughed. The boys were supposed to watch Joe, but where one twin went, so did the other. I didn't mind.

Mary lifted one leg after the other, in no hurry. "Come on, Joe" Mary said. "Do what I'm doing."

He rubbed his eyes and seemed too scared to move. Mary kept encouraging him. Joe moved one leg. He held it up in the air, almost falling over, but caught his balance.

"See," I said. "Now lift the other leg."

Joe swayed but lifted the other leg. Soon, he and Mary walked alongside me.

"Hold my hand," I told Joe. "And Mary, hold onto Joe's hand. We'll walk to the next tree together."

Mr. Henry set our harnesses underneath the tree with the cherry buckets.

"What are those?" Mary asked.

"The belts are what hold the cherry buckets against our bodies," I explained. "As we pick the cherries, we put them inside this bucket."

"And the bucket won't fall?"

"Right." I pointed to the wooden boxes. "Once your bucket is full, you dump the cherries inside the wooden box."

I clipped the buckets onto Mary and Joe's harnesses. Joe complained about how early it was and the weeds.

Mama and Aunt Louise called everyone for a short meeting underneath the first cherry tree. That's where everyone was given their quota for the day. The wooden boxes we had to fill were oblong with a wooden divider. Once they were filled, we'd stack them on top of each other. Mary and I worked on the same tree as Mama and Aunt Louise. The boys worked on a tree next to ours.

Our family picked cherries for what seemed like more than an hour and a half before taking our first break. Thomas and Joe spread the blankets next to each other.

Someone tapped my shoulder. It was Mary. She pulled me toward her. "You've been doing this since you were six?" she whispered.

I snickered. "Yep."

Mary wiped the sweat from her forehead and shook her head in disbelief.

Mama stood up and wiped her hands on her jeans. This was the only time that I had seen her in jeans or pants. She put her hat on, stood up, and said, "Well, let's get back to work."

Mary and Joe sighed and groaned as they stood up.

By the end of the day, I couldn't count how many trees our family had picked. The twins staggered to the cars. Joe leaned against one of my brothers and Mary against me.

Mama and Aunt Louise stopped a few feet from the car, near the hood. "You kids get in the car. We'll be there."

While in the car, I saw Mr. Henry talk to Mama and Aunt Louise. He gestured toward the cars, and paused before he paid them. This was different. Usually the money was counted and handed directly to one of them. Mama turned toward the cars and shook her head. Mr. Henry finished counting the money and handed it to Mama.

When Aunt Louise and Mama reached our car, they divided the money between the two of them. I thought Mama was gonna tell us what they talked about, but she didn't. Instead, she asked the twins how they felt about picking cherries. Joe and Mary didn't say much, which surprised me. This was, after all, their first day working in the fields. I think they were both scared to tell Mama the truth. Mary leaned her head against my shoulder while Mama drove away from the orchard.

Tuffy, our dog, woke us when we got home with his barking.

With the twins working, we would have two more to fight over who'd take the first bath. This time, Mama decided. "Mary and Maggie will take baths first," Mama said.

Edward and Thomas chose to wash up with the pump outside.

Mike said, "you and Joe can go next. I don't mind being last."

I sat in the bathtub, popping bubbles, thinking about my friends. Since our family worked the fields all summer, there was very little time for me to see Cheryl, Sarah, and Jackie.

Most of the summer, Jackie visited her uncle and aunt down south. Sarah worked on her family's farm. On Sundays, their family attended the Baptist church on the other side of town. Cheryl was my only friend who didn't have to work. Her father worked in the factory. She was the one I saw the most.

The phone rang. "Oh, Cheryl," Mama said with a jolly voice, answering it.

I stopped popping the bubbles and hopped out of the tub.

"How's the family?" Mama asked. "Good. Good." There

was a brief pause.

I reached for my towel.

Mama told Cheryl, "Maggie is in the tub and can't talk, but I'll tell her to call you."

Water splashed on the floor as I hurried to dry myself. "Mama, is that Cheryl?"

"Yes," Mama said. "I told her you'd call her back later."

I hurried out the bathroom, Mama had already hung up the phone.

"Remember, you have to set the table for dinner," Mama said.

After putting on jeans and a t-shirt, I ran into the kitchen and grabbed the plates from the cupboard, hoping to call Cheryl back before dinner.

"Maggie, please don't break any plates," Mama said. "We already don't have many that look alike. You kids have broken most of them. And one other thing. You know you can't talk on the phone until after dinner and the kitchen are cleaned up."

"Shoot," I mumbled. Those were the rules. We had to finish our chores before playing or talking on the phone. During the summer, except for Sundays after church, I didn't get to see

Cheryl much.

I placed the plates on the table and some silverware beside them. Mama was in the front bedroom.

. . . .

Tonight at the dinner table, it seemed unusually quiet. Normally, we would bicker back and forth. Maybe, we were tired from working in the cherry orchards today. My silence was from my growing impatience to call Cheryl. And I kept thinking about the beautiful lake we passed every day just before entering the cherry orchard. It was small with one side filled with marsh, while the other side appeared to be clear. If it was breezy, you could see the ripples coming toward our car. I didn't know how to swim, but at that time, swimming is exactly what I wanted to do.

"Maggie?"

"Yes," I answered, not sure who called my name. It surprised me when I noticed it was Mama.

"Maggie, I noticed you're not talking or eating much. Do you feel all right?"

"Yeah. I'm just not hungry tonight. May I be excused?"

"If everyone is finished eating, we can clean the dinner

table."

It was the fastest clean up that I had ever seen us do. We washed, dried, and put away the food in record time. Even Mama looked surprised.

Soon after, the boys went to their bedroom and the twins to the living room to watch TV. Mama walked toward the door.

I leaped out of the chair in th living room to catch her. "Mama," I asked. "Can I call Cheryl?"

"Yes, but don't be on the phone long. I'm just going over to see Aunt Louise."

I tried to call Cheryl, but her line was busy. Outside, there was a loud pop sound, followed by cheering. It sounded as if it was just out front.

Mike ran from the back bedroom and nearly knocked me over to look out the window. "Edward!" he yelled. "Grab the bat and ball."

Mike and Edward bumped into each other while racing to get out of the front porch. Mike yelled at the boys across the road, "Why didn't anyone come to get us?"

Joe followed Mike outside. Seconds later, Mike looked

back toward the house as Joe called out his name. "Watch out for the trucks and cars!" Mike screamed.

I went to the front porch and saw Joe in the middle of the road.

"Come and get him, Mike!" I yelled.

Mama was on Aunt Louise's front porch. She hollered at us for letting Joe get onto the road without help.

Mike hurried through the weeds to grab Joe's hand. Mike asked the boys again why no one came to get them. The neighbor boys waved their arms. "Just come on. We thought you guys were still eating."

As I walked back into the kitchen to make sure the food was put away, I heard drawers slamming and a loud voice from the boys' bedroom. I pulled the curtains aside, and there was Thomas. "Have you seen my lucky hat?" he asked. "The one with the ripped-up duck rim?"

"Why won't you guys let Joe play?"

"Because he'll slow the game down. He can sit on the grass and watch or keep score."

I felt bad for Joe and wanted to tell Mama. But if I did, the boys would get after me for tattling. I let it go and skipped outside to play hopscotch.

Before I could get out of the dining room, Mary asked if she could play with me. I thought of Joe and how the boys excluded him, so I said, "Sure. Come on."

Although Mary had asked to play, she sat on the top step of our house, watching. By the time I tossed the rock to the fourth square, she left the steps and mimicked me while I jumped.

"Can I play now?" Mary asked in a bashful voice.

"Is that why you practiced alongside me? You're not tired from picking cherries today?"

"Sort of," she answered softly. "But I don't want to be in the house by myself."

The twins were getting older and probably tired of playing with each other or watching television together.

"Open your hand," I said, "Here is the rock. Now be careful to toss it right here, on the first square."

Mary tossed the rock. She bent her knees. Her arms flailed and she jumped higher than necessary to the first square, and then to the second and third. At the fourth square, her eyes fixated to where she wanted to jump. I saw her lips move but couldn't hear what she was saying.

"Are you praying?"

Mary didn't answer. She jumped into the air and fell backwards. Her hands touched the third square, the tip of her tennis shoes on the fourth. Frustrated, she kicked the sand and ran underneath the weeping willow tree in our front yard that was next to the driveway where we were playing. She leaned against it with folded arms.

I ran to Mary, wrapped my arms around her in a big hug, and encouraged her to not give up. "Try again." I said. "We can jump together."

We walked back together while I told her a story. "When I was your age, I couldn't jump nearly as far." I said. She smiled.

"Mary, put the rock inside your hand and give it a toss."

The rock rolled past the first, second, and third square. Mary, seemed frustrated. I told her, "Now count 'one, two, three,' and jump." Mary stumbled and fell.

"Don't worry. Let's try it again, okay?"

This time, Mary took the rock, tossed it, and, without hesitation, jumped.

A loud honk sound from Uncle John and Aunt Pearl's house. Their house was on the other side of ours, separated by brush tall enough to resemble trees.

"Dang it," I said.

Mary stumbled again, arms in the air, as she tried her hardest to land on the fourth square. Her body froze. She leaned sideways for a second. "Look!" she hollered.

I turned around and saw that her feet were on the square. I was happy for Mary but curious about the honking coming from Uncle John's.

I ran through our backyard, near the chicken coop, to get a better look. "Darn it. I still can't see."

Another shortcut was to run toward the footpath that we all walked down to get to Uncle John's house and peeked around the trees. There was a car, but not one I recognized.

The driver's door opened. Uncle John had bought a brand new car: a shiny, red, four-door Cadillac. *This must be why he works all that overtime*, I thought.

Our family found many reasons to celebrate. Today, we celebrated Uncle John's new car.

"Let's all eat underneath the weeping willow tree," Aunt Louise said. "Ted, drag the picnic table over."

Soon after, Uncle John brought over card tables. All of us ate underneath the big weeping willow tree, laughing, joking, and enjoying each other. Uncle John drove his Cadillac onto the driveway that we shared with Uncle Ted for all to see.

After dinner, Tuffy wagged his tail, waiting for scraps. The grown-ups cleaned the tables. They told us not to go far and said that there would be an announcement. We ran to the backyard and hit pop-ups. That's what we called pop flies. Someone would stand back and try to catch each one.

Half an hour later, we heard someone hollering for us to come back across the road. Uncle Ted stood up and said, "I have an announcement."

We all looked at each other with a skeptical look on our faces.

"Tomorrow, Friday, there will be no cherry picking. We'll just enjoy each other."

We rejoiced, jumping up and down.

Once the sun set, we played hide and seek until Mama leaned out the back screen to tell us it was time to come inside.

46

Dear Diary,

Lots happened today. The twins picked cherries. I taught Mary how to walk through tall grass. Needless to say, she and Joe weren't too happy. At the end of today, we played hide and seek. We won't have to pick cherries tomorrow!

Chapter 21

The Chores

"Cock-a-doodle-do! Cock-a-doodle-do!"

I sat up in bed, frowning. "That darn rooster. Doesn't it ever think that when people get a chance to sleep, that's what they want to do?"

"Uh huh," my sister mumbled.

"It doesn't care, not one iota." I pulled the covers away and walked to the bathroom. There was one small window over the bathroom sink. I slid the curtains to one side but couldn't see that darn rooster. However, I did notice that Uncle Ted's red truck wasn't parked in their driveway. Then I remembered yesterday that he told everyone there'd be no cherry picking today, but the courthouse had added additional janitorial duties for him, so he'd be working.

By the time I came out of the bathroom, Mama had gotten up and was in the kitchen making breakfast.

"Maggie, could you please set the table?"

As the rest of my siblings came out of their bedrooms, Mama assigned other breakfast duties.

"Don't forget to look at the list of chores that I taped to the refrigerator door," she said.

Mike ran his finger down the list and stopped. "Mama."

"I know, Mike. You can keep an eye on the twins and make sure they finish their chores. She paused. "Maggie can help you."

"Mama," I whined.

"It's not much. I'm sure you don't mind, do you?"

"Okay."

The chores changed from week to week. The older kids were familiar with the list. When we didn't work the fields, a rule of thumb in our house was to wash up, eat breakfast, and check the chore list. Now Mary and Joe were a part of this ritual.

Mary frowned. After I put a plate on the dining room table for breakfast, I said, "Here, Mary, you can set this one right here. Now watch how I place the plates, silverware, and water glasses on the table."

Next, I walked her back to the list of chores. "Okay, all done. Put a big X next to it."

"Like this?"

"Yeah, just like that. See? Done." I pointed to the next thing. "After we eat, you and Joe will have to clean the dining room table, sweep the kitchen floor, and make sure all your clothes are put away. None can be left on the bedroom floor."

When I looked at Mary, she stood still. Her eyes weren't moving up and down the list. "You all right?"

Seconds passed. "This didn't seem like a lot of work watching you do it," she said in a soft voice.

I put my arms around her, "Once you do it a little bit, it won't seem much to you either. I promise. I'll help you."

Later, I saw her beautiful half-smile. She opened her hands and said, "Next plate."

Something my siblings didn't know was that ever since fifth grade, I had kept a diary. Probably nothing significant. I take that back. Yes, it was significant because they were all nosey. My diary was hidden in the bedroom that Mama, Mary, and I shared. There was an attic door next to the dresser that Mary and I shared. Mama didn't keep anything in the attic, and I wasn't sure what it was used for except as an excellent spot to hide my diary between the steps. Before I'd open the door to reach for my diary, I'd look over my shoulders to make sure no one watched. As quickly as possible, I'd open the door, reach underneath the steps, and slide my hand from side to side.

There were voices. I shut the attic door and pretended to look inside the dresser for nothing in particular. I peeked out my bedroom. Mary sat on the couch to watch a television show. I went back to the attic and reached for my diary.

My favorite spot to write was on the front porch, but before I could get comfortable in the over-sized chair, I heard a voice from the living room.

"Can I sit with you?" It was Mary.

"Sure," I said. "Come on."

She sat next to me and leaned her head on my shoulder. "You're always writing in that book."

"Uh hmm." I picked up my pencil and began to write.

"What do you write about?"

"Well, sometimes about what happened in school or about what happened during the day. Just about anything that comes to my mind." I began to write.

Mary asked, "What comes to mind now?"

Here's what I'm writing today:

"Dear Diary,

Our sixth-grade class was told we are moving down the hill, to the high school building, I'm not happy. Most of the class was surprised. We sat with our mouths open. The class had waited all year to move across the hall to be the first sixth grade class in the elementary school."

Mary had fallen asleep against my shoulder. As I gently tried to move her, my diary slid toward my knee. *Please don't wake up.* I decided to put her in our bed so that she faced opposite where I kept my diary if she moved.

With Mary asleep, the uncompleted list of chores on the refrigerator came to mind. I rubbed my fingers from top to bottom. The dishes were next on my list.

Thank God for my oldest brother. Whenever Mama wrote something on the list for me to cook, he'd switch with my list. Mama always told him, "When Maggie gets married, she won't know how to cook, and it'll be your fault."

"I don't want her to burn herself," he'd reply.

Mama shook her head and walked away.

It was dinner time. On the menu today was beans and

cornbread. Many times, I'd go to Aunt Pearl's for dinner, no matter what she was cooking. It sure wasn't beans and cornbread.

"Mama, is it all right if I go and eat at Aunt Pearl's tonight?"

She gave me that Mama look and said, "You don't have a taste for beans and cornbread?"

The smell of fried chicken and everything else Aunt Pearl was cooking - probably mac and cheese, collard greens, and cornbread was on my mind. With my hands already on the chair, ready to scuff it against the wooden floor, I had to be careful of my answer. With everyone's eyes on me, I replied, "Sure. Dinner smells so good. And besides, I enjoy our family conversations during dinnertime."

Edward looked at me with a smirk and his arms crossed, knowing I had just said one of the biggest lies.

"Mama, I have a question. You call Uncle John 'uncle,' and so do we. I'm not being smart-mouthed. I'm just still confused when I hear you call him 'uncle.'"

"My mama, who is your grandma, had two siblings, who are my Aunt Louise and Uncle John. Therefore, I call them 'aunt' and 'uncle,' and so do you. Does that help explain?"

"I guess so."

After supper, Mama asked us kids to double-check the list of chores.

"Mama, I've done all of my chores," I said.

"Then you can clean the table and put away the food. If anyone else has done all their chores, please wash the dishes and sweep the dining room and kitchen floors."

There was some grumbling, but everyone did what they were told. And, as if that wasn't enough work, we then had to go outside and feed the animals. We raised our own chickens and planted many of our vegetables - the same vegetables that I cleaned many Ball jars for to can, such as collard greens and string beans.

Mama got up from the table. "I'm going to take a nap. Don't let me sleep too long."

I rarely saw Mama nap. She was always doing something, like sewing us clothes, putting a button on my brothers' shirts, knitting, cooking, canning, and making sure us six kids were taken care of.

Two hours later, after doing all my chores, I wanted to sit in the oversized chair and write. I walked to the bedroom and stopped at the door. There Mama laid. She looked so peaceful, and she deserved every hour of sleep.

Since our daddy left and moved back to Chicago, Mama was the provider. I remember the stories Mama told us about our family. They lived next to each other down south. Once everyone had moved to Chicago, they bought a big house and lived together. Grandma cleaned rich people's houses and was paid very well. Mama wasn't used to welfare, yet here she was.

• • • •

With diary in hand, I walked to the front porch and sat in the oversized chair to write. The two-track road in the cherry orchard was on my mind today. I wrote:

The trucks or cars drive over and over the tall grass until a narrow two-track road is created. At times, there are cars that drive off the two-track road, leaving the tire tracks on the grass. Whatever we picked or topped, the roads separated the fields into sections. On the corner of each section was a wooden stake with a letter or number. Today we were in Section C.

"Charley Louise!"

I moved quickly out of the chair and went into the house. There was Aunt Louise, hollering for Mama.

Our families rarely locked the doors, except if we weren't home. We'd walk in and call out to whomever we were looking for.

"Charley Louise!"

I'd recognize that voice anywhere. I asked if something was wrong. "Where's your mama?"

Before I could call for Mama, she walked quickly out of the bedroom and asked Aunt Louise why she was hollering.

"Sorry if I woke you, but there is a job."

It was not news to us that Aunt Louise had found a job. She had been looking for a job for some time in the janitorial department at the Fremont nursing facility. Fremont and White Cloud were close to each other, and our family's name was well-known around the community, mostly in the fields, but also from cleaning houses around the lakefront.

"Inside the facility?" Mama asked.

"No," Aunt Louise said.

She told Mama that the director had approached her. Two of his friends were looking for someone to clean their summer houses around Robinson Lake before their arrival. There were two large homes. And Mama came highly recommended.

"The director wants you to call him with any questions as soon as possible," Aunt Louise said. "He'll be working late."

Mama called. She asked, "How large are the homes?" "How soon do the homes need to be cleaned." "What's the pay?" "Can I bring my older children?" There was silence until Mama said, "Um hmm."

When she got off the phone, I said, "Well?" The rest of the family was in the living room, waiting too.

Mama said, "The director told me that one house has five bedrooms, a study, living room, bathrooms, you know, the usual. The other has four bedrooms, a study, living room, den, bathrooms, etc."

A half hour later, the phone rang, and Mama was informed that no kids were allowed. I really wanted to go but also understood. This would be another source of income and possibly bring us closer to getting off welfare.

Robinson Lake wasn't far from our house. The lake was large, but because of the private homes, we didn't fish there. While Mama was gone, it was Mike's responsibility to watch us kids.

When Mama and our aunts left, Mike figured this would be the best opportunity to try our plan. There is a beach in White Cloud, but the Blacks didn't go.

"This is the perfect time," Mike said. "No Mama. And no Aunt Louise, who we all know sits in her rocking chair in the middle of the dining room to watch everything that happens."

"Plus," Edward said. "It's extremely hot today."

There was an open sandy area near the chicken coop. We all got shovels from the shed to dig the biggest hole we could. But every time we shoveled, the sand fell back into the hole.

"Why won't it stay in the hole?" I whimpered. "We've shoveled most of the day."

While we sat under the weeping willow tree to take a break, Mike hollered, "Hurry! Aunt Louise's car!"

Aunt Louise had come home earlier than we expected.

"Go hide the shovels inside the shed and act like we're playing. Hurry!"

Tuffy began barking as he ran alongside her car.

Mama walked toward us. We tried our best to distract her from the hole. We asked her about her day and to describe the house.

Mike began to holler, "Mama, let me show you something. It's in the house. A surprise."

The twins were supposed to watch for when they drove up, which probably was a mistake.

As soon as we thought we were in the clear, Mama stopped at the top step of our house. She looked at us, knowing something was up. She turned around. "Could you kids take the clothes off the clothesline?" She paused. She looked toward the middle of the yard and saw what was supposed to be a swimming pool.

"Mike!"

I didn't even know she could scream so loud. Mama was very light complected with freckles, but it seemed as though all her freckles had now disappeared. She continued to holler louder and louder. "Don't you kids know this is nothin' but poor man's sand, and no amount of water will last? If I had been driving, I could have driven this car into. . ." She pointed, wagging her finger. "Take those clothes off the clothesline, and you kids better fill this hole."

We continued to take the clothes off the clothesline. Later, Uncle Ted and Uncle John came to help us fill the hole. To add to our chores already on the refrigerator door, we all had to go into the garden and make sure there were no weeds growing, plus rake.

"Mama," I said. "Where do you want us to rake? Near the woods?"

My brothers told me to shut up. Mama gave me that stare. That Mama stare. Her eyes didn't more or blink.

Uncle Ted felt sorry for us and surprised the boys. He had built onto the already countrified basketball hoop behind the chicken coop. He put a new wooden pole into the ground with cement and bought a basketball net. When my brothers ran behind the chicken coop to play basketball, their mouths dropped open and their eyes were wider than a silver dollar. They jumped up and down in excitement. Sand scattered.

"I thought this might ease your pain," Uncle Ted said.

They ran to hug him as he handed them their new basketball. He stayed to watch them play for a short time and then walked over to his shop, which was next to the chicken coop, to put his tools away. Ever since Mama and Daddy separated, our uncles stepped in however they could to fill a void.

Dear Diary,

Our plan to build the swimming pool was a bust. We shoveled and shoveled but the sand kept sliding back into the hole, seeming to laugh at our every attempt. Mama came home and caught us in the act.

Chapter 22

The Ladder

Didn't matter that it was the end of school year. Our family had the same ritual. Over dinner, Mama told my brothers, my sister, and me that a decision had been made. This summer, once again, we'd pick cherries. But this time, it wouldn't be every day. Mama was offered a job at the Fremont nursing facility, possibly working Fridays. She wasn't sure if she would be working days or nights. The supervisor would work out the details and get back to her.

I dropped my fork, my mouth wide open. "Does this mean we won't -"

"That's right, Maggie. For now, you won't have to pick cherries on Friday or Saturday."

"Does this mean I'll be responsible for the kids?" Mike asked.

"Yes," Mama said.

"Even me?" Edward asked with a stern face.

"No. Not you Edward. You're old enough to watch after

yourself. Just don't wander off into the woods with your cousin, like you both tend to do, and bring a pocket full of snakes back with you."

Our cousin was Aunt Pearl's son, but not related to Uncle John. To my knowledge, he never finished school.

"What about me?" Thomas asked.

"Can you make sure you're not in some way or the other aggravating Aunt Louise?"

"And me, Mama?"

Mama turned toward me.

"Maggie, I know you're going into junior high. And I know you're a big girl. You can look after your little sister, but Mike will watch over you as well."

I hung my head. Mama put her hand underneath my chin and lifted it up. "You're a big girl, but don't grow up on me too fast, okay?"

I smiled and put my arm around my little sister.

With that decided, Mama reminded us that in a few weeks, on Monday, we would have to get up early, at 5:00 a.m.

Monday came around too soon. We rushed around the house.

"Someone get the lunches, water, pop, and ice chest!"

"Mike, hurry up!" Mama said. "And make sure everyone's out of the house before you lock the door."

He was always the last one out of the house, slamming the door shut.

. . . .

Everyone stood at their first cherry tree to begin work.

"Mama," Mike hollered. "The harness is too big for Joe. The straps are falling off his shoulders and the waist part is too big."

"Mary has the same problem," I said.

"Let me speak to Mr. Gill," Mama replied.

Mr. Gill walked in between the trees, not far from our family. Mama called him over.

"I know. I know. Harnesses for the two younger kids. This has happened to some other families. Let me take them to the shed and make a few adjustments. I'll be right back."

The shed was a short walk from our first row. In the meantime, Mama told the rest of us to begin picking. The twins picked cherries but put them into our buckets. It was a half hour before Mr. Gill returned with straps that could fit the twins. In order for the belts to fit around the twins' waists, Mr. Gill had punched more holes. He had done the same for the shoulder straps.

"Thank you, Mr. Gill," Mama said. "The straps fit just fine."

We worked over an hour until our first break. Mama called our names. "Edward, Mike, Thomas, David, Maggie, Mary and Joe. It's time for lunch."

Mama and Aunt Louise, who by now only worked sometimes, sat in the front seat of the car, their doors open. All of us kids sat underneath a tree on our blankets.

Thomas, the person who if everyone was going left, he'd go right, sat in between two of the lower branches of the same tree with a complaint after every bite of his sandwich. "I hate pickin' these damn cherries. Every summer, all we do is pick other people's damn crops, sweatin', not enjoying none of the summer."

I picked up a handful of cherries and tossed them his way. "None of us like pickin' cherries," I said.

"Shut up, Thomas, with all that cussin' before Mama hears you," Mike told him.

Thomas spoke in a nasty tone to me, tossing cherries back at us. "Maybe I'll tell Mama you cussed outside of church, and she'll wash your mouth out with soap."

Mama believed in the switch, belt, and a few other things to discipline. Sometimes punishment would could include raking the leaves behind the vegetable garden or pulling the weeds from the garden.

Mike didn't whip us, but with Daddy gone, and Mike being the oldest, most of us listened to him, except Edward, who was the second oldest.

Soon, we heard Mama and Aunt Louise slam the car doors. Next, we heard were the crushing of our lunch bags, voices from other families nearby, farm equipment, and the birds that flew above the trees chirping.

Thomas, who always had to say the last word, shut up, but not before he tossed another handful of cherries at my head.

I picked up some of them. "Let me see how juicy these taste."

"Both of you be quiet," Mike hollered with a stern voice.

There were times Thomas listened to Mike, but this was not one of those times. He tossed another handful of cherries and hit Mary.

She picked up the cherry and began to put it in her mouth. I immediately told her not to eat it.

"Why not? You did."

"You don't have to copy me. When I ate the cherry, I was being a smart aleck."

What I didn't know was Mama stood nearby and saw it all. "Time for everyone to get back to work. And remember, Maggie, to show Mary how to pick the cherries the right way and not squeeze too many."

Mary picked a couple of cherries at a time and put them in the bucket with careful attention. I didn't notice any that were squeezed.

Today, it seemed as though the boys got up and down the trees quicker, as though they were in a race. Sometimes that's exactly what the boys would do, trying to make some kind of fun out of work. This time, David, Aunt Louise's foster child, leaned the ladder against the tree branches before it was propped to make sure the ladder was stable against the branches.

We picked in sections around the tree. Mama hollered, "Remember to -"

"We know, Mama. Don't let the twins climb the ladders."

Laughter came from the other side of the tree. It was Mama and Aunt Louise.

Aunt Louise said, "Just be careful."

I looked up and noticed the tree branch sway as David hurried up the ladder.

"What happens if it gets windy comes and someone is up on the ladder?" Mary asked.

"Well, he has a few choices," I said. "He'd hang on as tight as he can to the ladder or branches or he might fall."

Mary flinched. "What? Fall?"

"Stop scaring her," Mike told me. "He won't fall."

"Mary, come closer. I remember when Mike climbed the ladder, playing that same game. The ladder wobbled as he tried to secure it onto a limb. The ladder moved even more. Mike grabbed onto a limb and hollered, 'Help! Help!'"

Mary's eyes got big. "What happened to Mike?"

"Edward grabbed that ladder, tryin' to move it closer to his body, but not before he fell on his butt."

"What?" Mary said.

"Maggie, stop scaring your sister. Less talk and more pickin'."

Mary picked the cherries and put them in her bucket. Every now and then she would look over her shoulder as Mike and David climbed up their ladders, branches moving.

"Come on, Mary. We have to pick a little faster," I told her.

Mary didn't respond.

After lunch, the family had picked cherries for three more hours when Mama finally blew her whistle. That meant quitting time. Everyone dumped the last bucket of cherries into the wooden container. Mr. Gill would come and check the containers. That's how we got paid.

"Mama, Mr. Gill's red truck is comin' up the path," I said.

Just like the first day when we arrived, his truck brakes squealed as his truck came to a stop. He got out, slammed the door, and straightened his cap.

Mr. Gill always, had a pencil tucked behind his ear and a small notebook in his blue jean jacket pocket. I couldn't count how many times Mr. Gill would lick his finger as he flipped the pages.

"I've counted some of the stacked crates between the trees and -"

"Yes, Mr. Gill," Mama said as she interrupted him before he could finish counting the crates.

"What I was trying to say is that your family worked hard today. Check to see if your numbers match mine."

Mama and Aunt Louise leaned closer to Mr. Gill. Both looked up and down the page. Once they agreed on the numbers, Mr. Gill pointed through the trees and told Mama we could get our pay at the office.

At the end of the day, Mama and Aunt Louise had to account for all the buckets and harnesses. Mr. Gill counted each one.

"Come back here, David," Aunt Louise hollered. "I need your bucket and harness before you open that door. We don't have all the equipment, they will deduct it from our pay."

When we got to the office, a lady stood outside, paying another family who worked in the orchard near us. She waved at Mama to drive forward.

Mama stopped the car.

"I'm the office secretary. Could I please see your ticket? You can hand the farm equipment to this man right here."

She walked back into the office and within a short time came to the car and handed Mama a white envelope. "Please make sure this adds up to what Mr. Gill told you."

Mama stood outside the car with Aunt Louise and counted the money. She looked up at Aunt Louise and nodded in agreement. "Yes, everything adds up," Mama said.

. . . .

I was awakened by a loud *'smack'* sound and voices yelling, "Run! Run!" As mama drove into our driveway after a long, hard day's work in the cherry orchard.

I rubbed my eyes. The neighbors who lived a few houses from ours were playing baseball in ole man Garrison's field across the road.

My brothers hollered out from the back window of the car, "What y'all doin' over there?"

Why he asked that, I don't know. It was plain as day they were playing baseball.

Mama honked the horn. I waved. "Come over! We're eatin' outside."

The boys' hollering out the window startled Mama and she pushed on the brakes.

"What's wrong with you boys? We could have had an accident."

When Mama parked, the boys couldn't wait to jump out of the car and run across the road.

Mike cupped his hands around his mouth and yelled. "Catch that pop fly!"

The boys ran across the road, Mama yelled at them again. "Get back to the house and clean up. After you wash up and we eat, then you can go and play baseball. Remember, you have to pack lunches for tomorrow."

While Mama gave the boys instructions, Mary and I to ran to the bathroom first. We filled the tub half- full with lukewarm water and Mary climbed in. The bathroom window was over the sink and open enough to feel a cool breeze. The wind was subtle enough for me to hear the leaves on the ground brush against each other. I stood on my tiptoes to open the window even more.

"Wow, Mary. The limbs are swaying back and forth as if they're playing their own baseball game with the wind." The sound was mesmerized.

Mary didn't respond. She played her game with the soap and water.

It didn't matter to me if she responded or not. There I stood with my fingers clamped against the window edge.

Mary was the first to bathe. As she had gotten older, I'd wait until she finished, and then I'd bathe in the same water. Today,

I chose to stare at the weeping willow branches and listen while the boys were fussin' over who'd be the first, second, third, or fourth in the tub outside to take their bath, if it didn't rain.

"Are you getting in the tub before the water gets cold?" Mary asked.

"Not this time," I answered. "I'll just wash up."

"Ooh. Mama's gonna get you."

"Why? Are you gonna tell?"

I turned around and saw Mary slip in the tub. One leg was in the air and the other inside. Mary gripped the side of the tub. Her face had a scared expression. She hollered. I turned around to help.

Mary held tightly onto my arms. Her fingernails dug into my skin.

"I thought I was gonna drown," she said.

"There's not enough water for you to drown. Next time just wait."

"I'm sorry." Mary shivered, still shaken from the slip.

Once she was out of the tub, I looked into her eyes. Mary held the towel tight around her waist. "You have to learn patience, okay?"

Mary nodded.

I gave her a big hug. "I'll always be there for you." I thought, *Thank God Mama isn't home.*

Since there were seven of us, Mama bathed at Aunt Louise's house. After working in the fields, she'd often walk across the yard to Aunt Louise's house because she had two bathrooms.

I grabbed Mary underneath her arms. "Why didn't you wait? You could have hurt yourself."

While Mary put on her clothes, I changed my mind and got into the same bath water. I leaned my head on the side of the tub, thinking about what I'd write in my diary. Mary surprised me by asking me to tell her one of my stories.

There was silence. This gave Mary a clue that I was thinking about what I would write in my diary. The same as what I'd do sometimes when sitting in the oversized chair on the front porch. At that moment, the boys ran into the house.

I heard Mike's voice outside the bathroom. "Maggie, when Mama comes back, tell her we went across the road to play baseball."

"Okay."

Inside our bathroom was a room separated by a curtain. That's where Mary stayed until she was dressed.

"What story are you gonna tell this time?" Mary asked.

"How about the ghost that lived upstairs in the attic?"

I opened my right eye just enough to see her reaction. Mary peeked around the curtain and in a soft voice she said, "Okay, but don't make it too scary."

"How can I tell a ghost story without it being scary? This is the perfect day, with the wind blowin' and all."

Mary hesitated. "Well, okay, but just a little scary."

With my head still resting against the side of the tub, I said, "This is the story of a ghost named . . ." I paused.

Mary came from behind the curtain with her clothes on. "How about we call the ghost Elliot?"

"Elliot?"

She was firm on the name Elliot, and I agreed.

"The floor in the attic creaked. Elliott's footsteps were heard as he walked downstairs. Before opening the attic door, which led to the bedroom, there was a knock."

"Knock. Knock."

Mama pushed the bathroom curtains aside. Mary and I jumped. Water from the tub splattered onto the floor.

"You were tellin' one of your scary stories again, weren't

you?" Mama asked. I didn't answer.

"Well, it's good you're getting out of the tub." I heard thunder. "Where are the boys?"

I let Mama know that I heard them fussin' about their bath, and then they ran across the road to play baseball. Mama hollered for the boys from the front porch.

"Mike, Edward, Thomas, and Joe, come inside. It's about to rain."

Just after she called them, the rain poured down, which made them happy because now they only had to wash up, but sad too because they couldn't finish their game.

"We were leading," Mike pouted.

Dear Diary,

It began to rain outside. My brothers weren't too happy because they had to come inside from playing their game. They also had to find the biggest pot they could to catch the water from the roof because it leaks all the time.

Chapter 23

The Weeping Willow Tree

Many times during the summer, the weeping willow tree became a place where our families ate dinner together.

Aunt Pearl and Uncle John brought her famous sweet potato pie with corn on the cob. Aunt Louise and Uncle Ted usually brought Kool-Aid mixed with lemonade and another taste that she'd never tell. All I know is that it tasted oh so good. Grandma and Grandpa brought salad with lettuce, cucumbers, and tomatoes grown in their garden. Mama brought the hot dogs, buns, and potato salad.

While everyone ate and laughed, slowly Mama stood up. She clapped her hands until there was silence. "I have an announcement."

Not that I wasn't going to pay attention, but I continued to nibble my corn on the cob while Mary sipped her Kool-Aid.

"As we all know," Mama said, "every time it rains, the boys run to grab the largest pot to catch the rain from our leaky ceiling in the living room where there is a big yellowish stain. Well, Uncle Ted let me know that he will work on fixing that leak, but the boys are gonna help."

Mike and Edward almost choked on their food. Mary spilt her Kool-Aid. I stopped eating but held onto the corn on the cob. With my eyes bugged out, I looked at the boys.

"But, Mama, we have no idea how to fix, patch, or whatever it is called, a roof," Edward said.

"Well," she extended the word. "Your Uncle Ted will teach you."

"When?" Mike asked.

"We're working on that part. But we can't continue to have one of you sleep on the couch with one eye open to make sure that the pot doesn't spill over."

Since Daddy and Mama had separated, the boys continued to have more grown-up chores. The added leaky roof chore wasn't written on the list. It would pop up whenever Uncle Ted called them over to his fix-it shop located in the back of his house.

Everyone began to eat again when I noticed Mama hadn't sat down. It was as if she wasn't sure what or how to say whatever was on her mind. She looked around at my brothers, sister, and me.

"Wait a minute. I have one other announcement."

Except for the trucks and cars driving by, there was silence. I prayed silently, *Please no onions* because they're topped into the school year. Then, as if a ray of sun shined down onto our table, Mama had a big smile on her face.

"Remember I told you kids about a possible job at Fremont nursing facility?"

"Yeah."

"Well, I wanted to announce that I will work in the kitchen on Friday nights. I will let everyone know the start date."

Our family jumped with joy. Tuffy, our Old English Sheep dog, jumped as high as the picnic table.

"Thank you, Lord," I said, "this year I won't have to smell like onions every day."

"Now, this isn't full time, but it is money," Mama said.

Our excitement grew and then ended when Aunt Pearl interrupted. "Those dark clouds are getting darker and darker."

That was the end of Mama's announcements. The boys helped Grandpa and Grandma. The rest of the family walked quickly to their homes. Aunt Pearl and Uncle John's house was the furthest away. Mary and I grabbed our food. We hurried back to pick up the napkins and table cloth. Once the food was put away, I went to my favorite place, the front porch, and sat in the oversized chair with my diary in hand. Mary followed and sat next to me.

As Maggie asked one question after another about the weather, I noticed she was growing into a very curious little girl. "What if it doesn't rain? Then what will we do? And how wet does the ground have to be for us to not work in the fields?"

A voice came from the doorway. It was Mama. "If I don't wake you up. That's the answer."

"Yay!" Mary said.

As usual, Mama was in the kitchen. I heard pots and pans clanking and smelled something she was stirring. Probably for Sunday's meal. She was the best cook in town.

I leaned over and whispered in Mary's ear, "If we don't work the fields or clean houses....Well, as much as I hate to top onions, it brings money into our house."

"But Mama -"

"Mary, we don't know the hours or when the job in the nursing facility will start. The job to clean houses around the lake isn't summer-long." I hugged Mary and noticed Mama look in our direction.

Mary leaned against my shoulder and continued to ask me about my writing.

"Believe it or not," I said, "I write better when it rains."

"How?" she asked.

"Close your eyes and listen."

"What we were listening to?"

"The *rain*," I whispered into her ear.

When a minute had passed, I told her, "Open your eyes and describe the sounds you heard."

Mary squinted at me. "Huh?"

"It's all right. If you'd like, you can still sit out here and watch me write."

Sometimes, Mama would ask us to make our lunches for the next day's work later in the day, mainly because if we made them too early, they would get eaten. Today, though, Mama changed her mind and told us this would be a good time for us to get ahead of ourselves. We used the bread Mike had taken out of the freezer yesterday.

It was like an assembly line with everyone having an assigned job. Mike made sure the peanut butter lid was screwed tightly onto the jar and put away.

After the sandwiches were made, I helped mix the Kool-Aid. Thomas encouraged me to put more sugar in it this time.

"Thomas, now you know good and well we have to measure the sugar, unless you're gonna chip in and help buy more with the money you make from the fields. You're the one who drinks most of it and puts the jar back in the refrigerator with only a sip left, saying, 'See? I didn't drink it all.'"

Thomas walked away.

With the chores completed, the boys went to their room. It sounded as if they were reading Mike's comic books. Mike loved comic books. Superman was his favorite. Every now and then, it sounded as if they were tussling. I could hear the beds scraping against a wall.

"Don't bounce on those beds!" Mama yelled.

Most of the time, the boys were outside, playing basketball or baseball across the road, but with the rain, there wasn't much for them to do.

Mama sat in the living room at the piano. This was one of her favorite things to do. She'd play whatever music the choir would rehearse for church. She had a beautiful voice but rarely sang lead for any of the songs. Sometimes Mary and Joe would sit beside her, singing, and she'd say, "Hit this key or hit that key."

Mama played and sang loudly until she was tired of the boys' noise from the bedroom.

"Mike, Edward, Maggie, Thomas, and twins! Come in here," she hollered. "Since everyone has so much energy, let's think of a game to play. Or we can practice the choir music for Sunday."

We quickly decided to play a game. No one wanted to practice the choir music. We played the game "I See Something." We'd pick an object inside the house with a certain color, raise our hands and Mama would pick the person to give the answer. We played until Mama felt we had settled down or tired out.

. . . .

"Do you think Mary will sleep tonight after you told her that ghost story?" Mike asked.

I brushed the question off and said, "Sure. It was a friendly ghost story." I turned away.

Mike replied, "I hope so, sis."

We went to bed and Mary seemed okay. I semi-slept with

one eye half-open before dozing off. During the night, I felt Mary toss and turn. Then she squeezed me. Gently, I removed her arm from around me. She squirmed a little but stayed asleep.

When I looked for Mama on the other side of the bed, she wasn't there. I rubbed my eyes. "Mama?" I whispered. I didn't see her sitting in the chair by the window in the bedroom either. Between the gaps of the curtains, I noticed it was daylight.

I tiptoed into the living room. At first, I didn't see Mama. She was sitting on the corner of the couch. I gently touched her arm. "Is something wrong?" I asked. "You didn't wake us for work."

"Earlier this morning, it was raining." Mama said. "The fields will be too wet."

I turned toward the bathroom.

"Wait a minute, Maggie. Are you sure that story you told your little sister wasn't too scary?"

Clearing my throat, I responded, "Yes, ma'am."

"Well, after you go to the bathroom, go and lie back down."

I gently moved Mary away from me, into the middle of the bed, and fell back asleep. When I woke up, it was 10:00. As I slipped into my house shoes, it sounded like commotion in the kitchen.

Mike and Edward were at the refrigerator. There was that darn list of chores. I squeezed in between them.

HOUSE CHORES

Mike   *Straighten your bed*

Feed the pigs

Make sure the twins have cleaned up and dressed

Wash dishes

Mop the dining room floor

Make sure everyone has sorted their clothes for the

  laundry

Edward   *Straighten your bed*

Feed the chickens

Mop the kitchen floor

Sort your clothes for the wash

Maggie   *Straighten the bed*

Sweep the living room floor

Make scrambled eggs and bacon for breakfast

Boil hot dogs for lunch

Sort clothes for the laundry (yours and Mary's)

Thomas   *Straighten your bed*

             Clean the bathroom

             Help Edward feed the chickens

Twins   *Mary, help your sister*

             Joe, help Mike

I heard Mama's voice from the living room, letting us know the rain had stopped, which meant the sun would probably come out later.

Mike told me, "I'll cook for you today, but you have to do one of my chores."

I crossed my arms, "Which one?"

"Uncross you arms," he said. "Ma is right. One day you'll get married and *will* have to cook. But, for now, you can wash the dishes for me."

I smiled. "It's a deal."

Edward walked toward me and bumped my shoulder. He mumbled, "Mike always helps you."

Mike pointed his finger. "That's the only chore I'll be doing for you."

"Agreed."

After coming out of the bathroom, I noticed the boys were

already sorting their clothes, the light colors from the dark. No matter what we did, it was always a contest. As they put their pile of clothes on the side porch, I called, "Hurry up, Mary! The boys are ahead of us."

My clothes were in the bathroom behind the curtain. Mary and I took our time sorting our clothes. While the weather might allow the boys' load to be washed and hung on the clothesline, I wasn't sure if all our clothes could be hung to dry. The boys had more people to sort, wash, rinse, and hang up their clothes. My thought process to win this race between me and my brothers changed. This was their race to win, for today.

Before any of the clothes could be washed, Mama called for me. She wanted to show me how much detergent and bleach to use. She reminded me that none could be wasted.

"Mary, reach up there for the detergent. I'll be right back with the bleach," I said.

"Mama," I hollered, "can I pour detergent in the water yet?"

"Yes, but don't pour too much. Use only one cup."

After I measured the detergent, the boys brought their white clothes and dumped them into the washer before Mama had a chance to pour the bleach. There were a lot of white clothes. I thought, *Maybe I should measure just a little more detergent.*

"How many cups did you measure?" Mama asked.

"One cup."

"Then stop! We'll have soap all over the ground."

Mama went to answer the phone. Mary and I watched the boys hang up their clothes like we were still competing. *Why must everything be a competition?* I asked myself. Mike waited for the first load to finish.

After answering the phone, Mama came back outside. "I see a lot of water dripping from the clothes," Mama said. "Why? And who put the clothes between the wringer of the washing machine? And who rinsed?"

"Mike you were in charge."

"I was watching the boys, but went to look for more clothes pins on the ground."

That left Thomas, Joe, and Edward to wash the clothes and hang them on the clothesline.

Mama pointed toward the clothes that had water dripping from them. She stepped in between the boys. "This is how you put the clothes through the wringer. Someone loosens up a shirt.

Slowly, begin to put it through the front of the wringer. Now, one of you stand from the back and slowly pull it through. Do the same after you rinse," she said. "If you clump them together, the wringer might unlock itself and nothing will go through, or not enough water will wring out of them. And what were you looking for on the ground?"

"All we found were broken ones, so we began to hang the clothes half folded over."

Mama thought that was a good idea. She asked if they had rushed to find the clothespins and if that's why they didn't find them all. By the end of Mama's tutorial, and Mary falling on her butt once after she pulled the clothes from the wringer, all six clotheslines were as full as could be.

I looked towards Mike thinking, *Mike had thought of the same idea as Mama, but didn't question her too much. He is truly maturing.*

But Mike wasn't the only one. The rest of us were either getting taller or more voiceful with our own opinions. Especially, Thomas. He and Aunt Louise seemed to always have disagreements. She'd ask him to help her with something. He'd do it, but not without mumbling. I remember one time she chased him across the back yard with a two-by-four. I don't know what he did, but he probably mumbled something he didn't want to do.

My little sister was close to her twin, but as she grew older, she began to follow me around. There were years difference between us. She was in early elementary and I was in the sixth grade. I liked to climb trees, talk to the chickens and pigs, and chase my brothers, which they hated. They could outrun me so I couldn't follow them, except for the time they jumped into the pigpen. I ran behind them, tripped over barbed wire, and got a big gash below my bottom lip. Boy was Mama mad. Mary couldn't run as fast as me and keep up. I'd find her sitting on the top steps as she waited for me with folded hands. After that, I was called a tomboy. My revenge to the boys was Mama's anger at them for leading me into the barbed wire fence.

The summer moved on. I used to have two rows of French braids, separated by what seemed like the largest part smack-dab in the middle of my head. Mama had braided my hair so tight that sometimes my head hurt. I'd try to loosen the braids. And, by then, my breasts had grown. I tried to hide them by wearing loosely fit tops. There was also my, well, the red spot, in the middle of my panties that seemed to come from nowhere.

Mary and I continued to play hopscotch, and the boys played basketball or baseball with the neighbor kids. It was funny and painful at the same time to see how the neighbor kids' friends who visited from the city adjusted to playing baseball in a field full of tall weeds with cardboard for bases. They would scrape their knees from the basketball games on dirt courts and want to quit. They learned to stop thinking they could outhustle my brothers with their city moves, and the same thing was true for my brothers.

Dear Diary,

My brothers and sister have grown. The school has told Mama that one twin will not pass to the next grade. Mama made the decision not to pass both.

Chapter 24

The Change

At the dinner table, Mama interrupted our meal with an announcement. Her announcements weren't uncommon, but tonight, her facial expression was different. She put her fork and knife down on the plate next to the mashed potatoes and pork chop that was partially eaten.

"Remember that I announced I'd be working at the nursing home in Fremont?"

"Yeah," we said in unison.

"I'll be working part-time on Friday nights. Aunt Louise will need a surgery. The facility has someone to work all her shifts but Friday, so I will be taking that night shift, starting immediately."

Someone gasped. This news meant that Mike would have added responsibilities to watch us younger kids: me, the twins, and, as best as he could, Thomas, because he always seemed to have his own direction. Edward, the second oldest, was more than capable of taking care of himself. Why Mama thought this was any different than any other day, we didn't know. Mike always watched after us.

"This means you will not have to pick onions, cherries, string beans, or anything else on Fridays or Saturdays. We will still fit in the church choir practice somehow," Mama said. "Also, boys, your uncles will want to work with you to patch up that roof. My guess is probably on a Saturday since that will be the time everyone is home."

"Okay," Mike and Edward answered. "Thomas?"

He looked at Mama with a smile.

"You can help," Mama said.

Thomas' smile turned quickly into a frown.

After dinner, Mama called me into the bedroom. I wasn't sure why.

"I noticed, in the wash, a red spot on your panties."

We both sat on the bed. She moved next to me and put her arms around my shoulders. It was our first conversation about the birds and the bees. I just said, "Mama" and sighed.

"You'll be in junior high this fall, and the boys might look at you differently. You might get nudged, or someone might say 'hi' who hasn't said 'hi' before."

I sighed again. "There's nobody that I like."

"Let me show you how to put a tampon napkin on with the strap and how to douche."

The more we talked, the *more* my stomach hurt. "First," I said, "if you haven't noticed, are my enormous breasts. And now this?"

"Yeah. We can both speak to the church mother after the service on Sunday."

I went to the front porch to write in my diary. The old cushion we sat on had flattened. Mama had surprised me with a larger one that she had sewn.

Mary came to the front porch and stood.

"Sit down, Mary," I said, "right here next to me."

For the first time, she held up her own diary. We smiled at each other. "Are you sure I can sit next to you?" she asked.

I nodded.

She sat down and began to look around outside.

"What are you looking for?" I asked.

"Remember you told me to listen to the sounds and see my vision."

"Okay. So, what do you see?"

"There's a bird's nest in that tree."

"What tree?"

She pointed to the left of the porch. "See it?"

"So, what will you write? No, don't tell me. Just write."

Mary and I sat next to each other and wrote in our diaries. I tried to peek and read hers but couldn't understand some of it. The words didn't seem to connect with each other, but that didn't matter. She was writing.

There was a horn sound in our front yard. Usually, we could see who turned into the driveway, but with the way our front porch was positioned, we couldn't.

"Maggie," Mama called. "It's Cheryl."

When I walked into our living room, there wasn't just Cheryl, but her brother too. He smiled. I smiled. Mama didn't. This is what she was talking about: boys.

"Come on, Cheryl," I said. "Mary and I are sitting on the front porch."

"Daryl," Mama said. "The boys are in their room. Mike, Thomas, and Edward, Daryl is here. Why don't you boys go across the road and play baseball?"

Mary looked at the floor, shy. She walked past Cheryl and sat on the couch, her doll in one hand and diary in the other.

Cheryl and I sat in the oversized chair, squished, but we didn't care. She watched the boys as they walked across the road and giggled. Mary was sitting by herself, not writing in her diary.

"Cheryl, do you mind if Mary sits with us?"

We looked at Mary. "No, I don't mind," Cheryl whispered. She smiled.

"Where can I sit?" Mary asked.

"There are cushions right here." Cheryl moved them to form a half circle.

During our phone conversations after school was out, Cheryl and I had put together a list of things we'd like to do over the summer, whenever our family didn't work in the fields, such as going over to each other's houses, possibly staying the night, making our hopscotch games more fun, and junior high school. As we read the list, Mary sat with her head between her hands.

"Mary," I said. "Can you think of anything?"

"Are you kiddin'?" She had the biggest smile. "Really?"

"Yes," Cheryl and I said in unison.

"But you'll have to sit on the cushions," I said. "Only

because there's not enough room in this chair for all three of us."

Cheryl said, "You know, Mary, we can share sitting on the cushions sometimes and you in the chair, if that's all right with you."

By the time we got to the bottom of the list, Mary asked, "Can I add anything? I mean anything?"

"Sure."

We heard an argument. We stood up and looked across the road. The boys were debating as if someone was tagged out. Someone yelled that they weren't.

Our brothers were serious about baseball games. It's not as if any of them will be drafted by the Dodgers or Cubs, but who am I to diminish their hopes and dreams. They were used to playing in tall, grassy fields, or weeds, as we called them, that went up to their knees. That made it hard to see where the ball rolled.

I felt a tug on my arm. It was Mary. With her soft-spoken voice, she asked, "Can we please go back to our diaries?"

"Now, we might not be able to meet every week, but what about after church service?" I asked. "Sometimes, you know, we have night service, YPWW, or dinner in the church kitchen. We can sit on a blanket underneath the big apple tree next to the church."

"Mary," I said. "There is a wooden box on top of our dresser. Look inside and grab a handful of paper and three pencils."

"Three?" Mary asked.

"Yup. Grab three."

She ran inside as if there was a fire, bumping into the arm of the chair next to the bedroom door.

"Slow down before you hurt yourself," I said. "It's in the same box where Mama keeps the lined notebook paper for school."

While Mary went to get the paper and pencils, the boys continued to fuss over their baseball game. Uncle John ran across the road. We couldn't hear every word, but he waved them over. Then he pointed toward the houses.

Uncle John must have told them to stop all the fussing or they'll go inside the house because the boys walked to their bases. Someone kicked the weeds. Another boy threw his glove on the ground and then picked it up after Mike was able to run home and score.

Uncle John continued to monitor the game.

"Here's the box," Mary said, handing it to me.

Everyone had a pencil and diary. I looked around before writing, hesitant, because the red spot in my panties lingered in my mind. I wanted to talk to Cheryl about it, but not Mary.

Mary blurted, "What should we write about?"

That got me out of a jam, I thought.

"We can write about anything?"

"Yup," I said. "Anything. Remember how I encouraged you to close your eyes? Listen to the sounds, or maybe write about what happened in your life this week."

"How about this week?" Cheryl asked. "Did you do anything exciting?"

Soon the only noise we heard was the boys' baseball game across the road and Mama playing the piano. The three of us just wrote. Mary took a little longer because she couldn't write as fast.

"I'm finished," Mary said.

"Finally," I said. "Mary, there's nothing on your paper."

"I can't write that good."

"Let me help you."

"This week, I picked cherries," Mary said. She looked up at me. "But you helped me a lot."

We smiled and hugged each other.

"See," I said. "You wrote your first diary entry. Well, almost your second. This is for you to keep and put where no one can find it.?

After I helped Mary, Cheryl and I read from our diaries. Like yesterday, it began to sprinkle, but not enough to go inside the house. The boys often played in the rain, so a few sprinkles weren't going to stop them. Uncle John stood in the sprinkles with them.

Half an hour later, it started to storm. Mama leaned her head against the doorway of the front porch. "It's time to come in. Tell the boys ...." Mama paused. She looked across the road. "Never mind. I see Uncle John over there."

"Another day of picking cherries or topping onions might be canceled?" Mary asked.

"Yeah, but remember, today is Saturday, and tomorrow is Sunday."

The boys ran with Uncle John to the house.

"Since your mama has taken a job with the Fremont facility, how do you guys know when you'll have to work in the fields?" Cheryl asked.

"Usually, we will have a meeting at the dinner table."

Mama turned off the television set. This was normal within our family whenever there was lightening. She sat in her room to read her Bible. Cheryl, Mary, and I were in the living room playing a game of tic-tac-toe. The phone rang. I ran to answer it and stopped, making sure it was our ring. We shared a phone with what is called a party line, which connects several houses to our line. I had to wait for two rings with a pause and two rings again.

"Hello?"

"Hello, Maggie. Could I please speak to your mother?"

"Mama," I called. "It's Cheryl's mother."

"Praise the Lord," she said. She took the phone from me. "How can I help you?"

Afterwards, Mama let Cheryl and I know that her mother would be over once the weather cleared. We smiled and kept playing tic-tac-toe.

Two hours later, we heard a car horn outside our house.

"I hope the kids weren't any trouble," Cheryl's mother said.

"No. Not at all."

Cheryl walked toward the door and called for her brother. "Where's that ugly brother of mine?"

"I don't know what she's talking about." He said. "I'm the oldest, and handsome." He looked toward me.

I watched him walk out the door. Once he was outside, I ran

to the bathroom to stare out the window and catch a glimpse of him before his mother drove out of our driveway.

. . . .

Living in a small town, there wasn't a lot of excitement. A lot of it was self-made fun. Sitting on the front porch with Cheryl and my little sister was more exciting to me than any work our family did in some farmer's field.

Every now and then, Daddy would call. Mama hung up the phone in sadness with no one to share her bed but my sister and I. Writing in my diary was my safe place. Today, when Mary and I sat on the front porch to write in our diaries, something seemed different.

I walked through the house and called for Mama. She wasn't in the bathroom, in the bedroom, or in the front yard, working in her flower garden.

I walked into the boys' bedroom. Mike wiped sweat from his forehead. "It's so hot," he said.

"Have you seen Mama?"

Mike walked into the kitchen. "She's in the backyard, checkin' on the chickens." He reached for a glass out of the cupboard. "We had to fix the coop."

I peeked out the back porch windows. Just like Mike said, there she was with Uncle Ted. The chicken coop was close enough so that I wouldn't have to run out to let her know we'd finished our chores. I stood on the top step of the back porch, one hand holding the screen door open.

"Mama?" I yelled.

She came from the back of the chicken coop.

"Mary and I finished the dishes. Can I call one of my friends to come over?"

"That's okay. Which one?"

"Um, Cheryl."

Mary seemed to enjoy hanging out with me and Cheryl. She beat me into the house to the phone.

"Can I call?" she asked.

Although Cheryl was my best friend, it seemed as though she had accepted Mary to write with us. "Sure. You dial. Here's the phone number." I caught her finger before she dialed to remind her how Mama taught us to talk on the phone and to say hello to her father or mother if they answered.

By the time Cheryl arrived, Mary had put out the writing

board and her diary. She sat on the cushion. Cheryl stood in the doorway. "Wow, someone's ready to write." Mary grabbed her pencil.

"Is something wrong?" I asked.

Cheryl sat down in the oversized chair. "I wondered if we could change from our usual plan of writing in our diaries and play hopscotch or something else?"

Mary put her pencil down and looked up at me.

"Mary, could you see if there is any more Kool-Aid in the refrigerator?"

After Mary left, I asked, "Cheryl, is there something wrong?"

She glanced back toward our kitchen. "I just don't feel comfortable talking about my boobs, first bra, and boys with my little sister around. Is that bad?"

Mary came back. "There's no Kool-Aid."

"You know what," Cheryl said. "How about we write something first, but only two lines, and then play hopscotch?"

Mary's smile came back. Cheryl wrote her two lines, and so did I. Then helped Mary.

Cheryl tried her best not to hurt Mary's feelings. It was a

good idea to make our writing only two lines so that it wouldn't take long for us to read to each other. We giggled laughed at Mary's diary voice, not to make fun, but because she was so cute when she read. And then we clapped. She smiled.

"Maggie?" Mama yelled. I'd heard that tone before. It meant something was wrong.

"Here I come."

"How come all of the dishes aren't put away?"

Mary had helped me with the dishes. When I looked near the stove, I noticed she had left some of the pots and pans out.

"I'll put them away now."

"Let me help," Cheryl said.

While we worked, we talked about what to do from the list we had put together. Cheryl brought up hopscotch.

"You must really like hopscotch," I said, "You keep bringing it up."

Mary didn't say anything. I think she pretended not to hear. She wasn't good at hopscotch. She had practiced with me but became frustrated when she couldn't jump past the third square. Cheryl didn't know that.

"How about jump rope?" I suggested.

Cheryl and I began to walk out the door. When we turned around to close it, Mary stood in the dining room, in our view. Cheryl and I looked at each other. We opened our arms and said, "Okay." All three of us hugged.

"How about we do both," Mary said.

The jump rope was usually tied around the big oak tree in our back yard, but we didn't see it.

"Maybe I put it on the back porch?" I said.

"I'll look," Mary said.

"You know what, Maggie? It might be all right for Mary to hang around us this summer," Cheryl said. "After all, she doesn't have anyone else."

Mary and I were separated only by age. I was in junior high. Mary was in fourth grade. She was a quiet, thin girl who was self-conscious because she didn't have as much hair as me. No matter what different remedies Mama tried, from blessed olive oil to prayer, Mary's hair wouldn't grow. And no matter how much I told her that her hair didn't matter, she wore hats. Her favorite hat was dark blue with an embroidered sunflower on the front. Mama brushed Mary's hair flat and French braided the front because it wasn't long enough in the back for braids. I thought, *if only I could give her some of my hair.*

Mary ran out of the house, excited. "I found the rope. It was behind a box on the porch."

First, we played single jump rope. Mary was pretty good, but we had to slow down the rope turns. She didn't jump as fast as Cheryl or me.

"Mary, how about double Dutch?" I asked.

She looked unsure. "I guess so. That's with two ropes instead of one, right?"

"Yeah," I answered. "I'll help you jump."

"Who will turn the other end?"

"Uncle Ted put a wooden prop on the tree," I said. "That way we can single twirl or double wrap the rope without it sliding down the tree."

When Mary saw how it worked, she asked, "Will you still help me, Maggie?"

"Sure. Just watch me."

Cheryl turned the rope. It hit the grass, but not enough to disrupt our jumping. I noticed Mary mimic me. When I jumped on one foot, she'd do the same. Sometimes it was funny to see her efforts, but we tried hard not to laugh.

"Okay, Mary, do you want to try?"

It was hard to hear her. "Yes," she said.

"Let's stand in the middle together. Take my hands. When I say, 'Jump,' you jump." I noticed she was paying close attention. "Okay, Mary. One, two, three, jump in."

Her feet got tangled in the rope. She looked defeated and scared.

"That's all right," I said. "It took me a long time, and many tries, to learn too. Let's try it again. One, two, three, jump in."

"Mary," I said, "you did it!"

"I know," Mary said.

She put her hands over her mouth. "But I stepped on the rope."

"That's all right," Cheryl said. "You jumped your first double Dutch!"

"Let's try again," I said.

"No, not right now," Mary said. "I might mess up. I want to remember what I've done. Let's go back to singles."

We told her we'd like to make a different game out of the single jump. With a huge smile, she nodded. The rules were to see who could jump the longest without stopping the rope.

Mary wanted to be the first to jump. I twirled the rope slower and allowed her three times to not stop the rope.

"Cheryl," I said. "We've been friends for a long time, and I love that you live right next to our church."

Mary stopped jumping. "Are you guys paying any attention?"

"I'm sorry, Mary."

We stopped playing and sat under the weeping willow tree, tossing anything we found into the air. Cheryl and I told Mary that we enjoyed her company.

Cheryl hugged Mary and said, "You are the little sister that I never had."

Dear Diary,

Today was a good day. My little sister learned how to jump double Dutch, and our sisterly bond grew stronger.

Chapter 25

To Be or Not To Be

The Bible is where we wrote our family tree. At the top was Grandma and Grandpa, and then our grandma's brother and sister's family, Uncle John and Aunt Louise, with their family names. Charley Louise Dorsey, our Mama, was the daughter to Grandma and Grandpa.

I remember Mama telling us, "This way, the family will always be kept close to God, and you children will know who you're related to in this world." But for me, the one person's family that will always be missing is Grandaddy Charley's. I still don't know them.

. . . .

Mary wasn't feeling well today. I sat on the front porch writing thoughts in my diary. Cheryl had gone down south to visit her cousins. That's what made me think of my family. The more time that Mary and I spent together, the closer our bond became, including with Cheryl, while writing in our diaries. But sometimes I wanted to keep my thoughts to myself. At times, I felt torn between the attention I gave to Mary versus Cheryl.

Sweat rolled down my forehead. I wiped it away. This morning seemed hotter than at the fields, but that didn't matter. It was Sunday and everyone went to church today with no complaint. Mama figured we could pick crops, come home and run across the road to play baseball or basketball in the backyard, then we could go to church.

As Mama drove the car into the church parking lot, I became anxious. Not necessarily for church, but because my best friend would not be next door.

The choir lined up in the kitchen. Even though I knew Cheryl wasn't home, I peeked outside the kitchen door toward her house.

"Maggie!" Mama called.

"Get inside. The choir is about to march into the choir stand."

I closed the door slowly.

"Geez," Mike said. "It's not like she died and went to heaven or somethin'."

I rolled my eyes at him. He just walked away. As the choir walk into the sanctuary, I noticed guests who sat in the pew next to Missionary White: a mother, father, boy, and girl. During the sermon, I noticed the little boy rest his head against his sister's shoulder. Every time she shoved him away, his head would move back and rest on her shoulder again. I snickered.

The pastor announced, "Immediately following the service, dinner will be served. Please be mindful and allow any visiting pastors, deacons, and the missionaries to be served first. Thank you, and God bless."

"I'll never get used to going to church," the boy visitor whispered to his sister.

"Just to let you know, I heard what you said." I whispered to them.

They turned around to face me and frowned.

"Why not?" I asked. "Church isn't all that bad."

"Because the service is too long," the boy said. "The Church of God In Christ has long-winded preachers."

"Yes, agreed." I leaned against the wall.

"It doesn't seem right to hold services so long in this heat," he said.

I asked, "Are you in town as visitors, or are you moving to White Cloud?"

"We're visitors with Missionary Long, our grandmother."

"Oh. My name is Maggie, and this is my sister, Mary."

"I'm James, and this is my sister, Janet. We're from down south. This town seems awfully small to have so many churches. When our family drove through town, I counted each one."

I laughed. "How many did you count?"

"There is a Catholic church, Methodist, Baptist, and your church, The Church of God In Christ."

"That way people can attend whatever church they want," I said. "My friends Jackie and Sarah go to the Baptist church across town. But my friend Cheryl doesn't attend church, and she lives right next door, on the other side of the fence."

On Sundays, Cheryl would sometimes cut across the back field of her house, hop over the fence, and wait for me underneath the big apple tree on the church's property.

"Maggie, would you please go out to the car and get that bag sitting on the floor?" Mama asked. "It's right by the front seat."

"Shoot. Mary, save my spot in line. I'll be right back." I let the screen door to the kitchen slam.

Once I handed Mama the bag, I walked quickly back to my spot in line. There was a table right next to the door. "Mary, hurry up and grab those seats right there." I pointed.

As fast as we could, we ate our food. Everyone wanted to go outside.

A few of us played baseball behind the apple tree, and some chose to climb the tree. Then we heard James holler.

"You all right?" I asked.

"Yeah. The screen door slamming scared me."

Under the tall grass lay a piece of paper.

"What is that?" I said.

I looked up, and there was Cheryl. My eyes got as big as two silver dollar coin. "What are you doin' here?" I asked.

"Well ..."

We screamed with joy and jumped up and down.

"Let me finish," she said. "Once we got down south, I asked Daddy if I could come back with him. After all, he drove down south to drop off Mama and my brothers. They talked it over and decided I could come back home with Daddy. I just have to do a lot of the housework by myself. But here I am!"

I introduced Cheryl to James and Janet and told her about

the letter we found under the tall grass.

"Remember the letter Miss Carol gave to all of the students in our fifth-grade class at the end of school year?"

"Yup. Why?" Cheryl unfolded the paper. "The letter. I must have dropped it one Sunday when we played under the apple tree."

"What's so important about that letter?" Janet asked.

Cheryl crossed her eyes at her.

I had to do something to break up the uncomfortable feeling in the air. "As I said earlier, Cheryl, Janet and James are guests, visiting one of the missionaries of the church for the summer. They're from down south, like your family."

That didn't seem to help like I thought it would. " Cheryl," I said. "There's a blanket in our car. Come help me get it. We can lay it underneath the tree."

When we reached the car, I asked Cheryl, "What's wrong? This isn't like you. You're my best friend. Nothing, or no one, can take that away."

"Yeah."

"James and Janet are guests only for a short time."

Cheryl moaned. "Yes, Maggie. I know."

"Could you please try and get along?"

Cheryl sighed. "Okay. I'll try harder."

We walked back with the blanket and spread it underneath the tree. "I thought it might be good to sit on the blanket instead of the tree branches. That way none of us will get our church clothes dirty."

Everyone sat down, except James. He leaned against the tree, defiant. Cheryl silently reread the letter.

James and Janet asked again about the letter.

Cheryl read the letter. "Dear Class: This is to inform you that the fifth-grade class going into the sixth grade will be a part of the White Cloud Junior High School in the fall."

She folded the letter and put it inside her pocket. "Maggie, you know that means. We'll be in junior high."

"What's wrong with that?" James asked.

"It's junior high school. That wing was for the fifth and sixth graders, or so we thought." Although we had already talked about this disappointment, it felt good to talk to other young people about it.

"Keep talking then."

"You guys," Cheryl said, "going down the hill would be a big jump. We thought we would be the upper classmen. But no.

There will be the 'I think I'm prettier and more popular' girls to deal with. The fifth and sixth graders, we had our own hallway. It was supposed to be our time to be the popular ones."

"So the last day of school, your teacher gave you guys that letter?" Janet asked.

"Um-hum. We were told to give it to our parents and not open it," Maggie said.

"Don't tell me you opened the letter," James said.

"Yeah, but I folded it back like the teacher gave it to me," Maggie said.

"Me too." Cheryl smirked.

"At any rate, that's not the real problem," I said, "The real problem is we're now in junior high with all the snobby girls, who will be upper classmen to us. Do you guys understand?"

Janet said, "Kind of." She continued to pick at a loose piece of cotton from the blanket.

James nodded his head and smiled.

Cheryl and I mumbled to each other, repeating, "We waited all year."

"Well, it's not gonna help to keep whining about it," Janet said. "The decision has been made. You're moving to the sixth grade, no matter what. Where we live, our sixth grade has always been part of the junior high."

"But this is *our* experience," Cheryl said. "They shove us in the bathrooms at the football and basketball games, and now we'll have to see them every day."

"Imagine being down south where you're outnumbered and already not accepted," Janet said. "You just came from down there. Why did you decide to come back?"

With a soft tone, Cheryl said, "I'm sorry. You're right. My experience is not the same as yours."

As I listened to Cheryl and Janet, I decided my goal this summer would be to help mend their relationship.

· · · ·

This Sunday, our church service ended at 3:30. The choir, row by row, walked inside a room behind the pulpit to hang up their robes.

In the room, my brothers played around. One hung up his robe while the other knocked it down.

"Mike, Edward, Thomas, and Maggie!"

Mama said our names as if she was calling roll. We immediately stopped what we were doing.

For some reason, Mama seemed in a hurry to get home. She abruptly stopped the car approached the church entrance, preventing her exit.

I rolled down the front window and rested my arm on the open edge. Cheryl sat in her front porch swing and waved. I waved back, all the while wondering how to mend her and Janet's relationship.

That night, after preparing for work tomorrow at the cherry orchard, Mama asked everyone to meet her around the dining room table. "Aunt Louise called. She wanted to let us know that we'll be one person short tomorrow."

We looked at each other, around the table wondering who was sick. Mama said, "It's Lewis." Lewis, is Aunt Louise's adopted son. "Everyone, let's clean up. Mike, make sure Joe has brushed his teeth before going to bed. And please don't stay up late."

Mary put on her pajamas, sat in the middle of the bed, and listened as I read one of my many short stories until she fell asleep. Mama sat on the bench in front of the vanity. I watched as she snapped the last pink roller in her hair, reached for a silk rag, and wrapped it around her head.

"Mama, could I talk to you for a minute?"

"Are you all right?"

"Yes, health-wise, but I have another concern. Cheryl was supposed to stay down south with her brother and mother for a month but came back home with her father."

"Is that the problem?"

I scooted closer to Mama. "The problem is between Cheryl and one of Missionary White's granddaughter, Janet, who is visiting for the summer. After church, when we all sat under the apple tree, they began to argue."

"Um-hum," Mama said. "Tell me more."

"Cheryl and I were talking about the letter our teacher gave us about the sixth grade moving to the high school building. Janet said something to Cheryl about the letter, and then Janet ended up walking away. I was trying to figure out what I could do to keep the peace when they visited our church."

When Mama put her comb down, I moved closer. "Next Saturday, I want to invite Cheryl over to our house ... and Janet."

Mama pulled strands of hair from her comb and tossed them into the trash can. "A good friend is hard to come by, especially a best friend, so I think that's a good suggestion."

I quietly hugged Mama. "What about Mary? She's been

hangin' around Cheryl and me a lot."

Mama said, "She can spend some time with me while I run some errands in town."

I like that idea. "I'll talk to Cheryl and call Missionary White tomorrow after we come back from the cherry orchard."

"Maybe I should call Missionary White," Mama said.

"Yeah, that's probably better if the invite comes from you."

"Now, let's go to bed," Mama said. "We have to get up early."

I woke up with energy and wanted the day at the cherry orchard to fly by.

Mama pulled into the road to the orchard. Mr. Gill waved for Mama to stop the car. "I'm moving your family from the usual orchard to another one," he said. "Follow me."

We drove behind Mr. Gill to another part of the orchard that hadn't been picked. Our family had a pattern of how to finish a row to get to a certain stop point. Now, all that changed.

Mr. Gill noticed we were one person short and wanted to make sure we could still work at the same pace. Mama and Aunt Louise reassured him there would be no problem.

Mr. Gill hesitated. "And please don't let the young ones run off. This is a large piece of land, and we don't want anyone to get lost."

"We'll keep an eye on them," Mama said.

"What's your hurry, sis?" Edward asked. "Last I remembered, you hate coming to the orchards."

It didn't matter to me what Edward said. I ignored him, grabbed Mary's hand, and strapped our cherry buckets around our waists. I encouraged Mary to pick faster. She looked at me and noticed something was wrong. I didn't want to hurt her feelings by letting her know she wouldn't be with me and Cheryl on Saturday.

Today was extremely hot. Mama noticed how fast I filled my buckets and asked me to slow down. "Drink plenty of water," she said. That gave Edward his opening to do his usual tease, with me teasing back, until Mama stepped in.

"Both of you stop," Mama said. "You're always picking at each other. We're here to pick cherries."

Mama was right. I slowed down a little.

Mary began to question me on my silence. I felt terrible not letting her into the secret about Cheryl and Janet.

"Are we still gonna write in the diaries?" She asked. "How about double Dutch? You can teach me to jump better."

"Time for lunch," Mama hollered.

Thank God. Right on time.

After lunch, the day went faster. At 3:00, Mama let us know it was time to quit and go home. She asked everyone to pick our last bucket of cherries.

Mr. Gill met with Mama and Aunt Louise. He flipped the pages of his notebook and continued to write. "Okay, Louise, here are the number of cherry boxes. Is that correct?"

Mama moved her finger up and down on the pages of the notebook while Aunt Louise looked over her shoulder. "Yes, that's what we counted."

When the office secretary paid Mama, we got in the car. Mama couldn't get home soon enough as I anxiously waited to call Cheryl away from Mary's ear.

When we got home, Mama said, "I'll take my bath at Aunt Louise's house. See you kids soon."

I tripped, and Mike and Edward beat me into the house and to the bathroom. Edward stood guard outside the door. Thomas decided to follow Mama to Aunt Louise's house and wait for one of their bathrooms, not wanting to bathe outside in the tub or with the hose.

Mary went with Mama to Aunt Louise's house, giving me the perfect opportunity to call Cheryl. Her phone was busy. I waited impatiently and called her number again. This time it rang twice before her father answered.

"Hello, Mr. Hardiman," I said.

"Well, hello, Maggie. How is your mother?"

"She's doing fine."

"You probably want to speak to Cheryl. I'll get her."

"Yes. Thank you."

Cheryl answered the phone, but she didn't sound the same.

"Are you feelin' all right?"

"Yes. Just a little somethin' with my throat."

"Oh. I was wondering if you'd like to come over to my house this Saturday afternoon."

"Yes, are you kidding me? Wait a minute. Will your church friend be there?"

I let Cheryl know that Janet would, but not her brother. Our family was on the welcome committee at church. Now, it wasn't that I volunteered to be on this committee, but Mama signed us up for just about anything and everything at church.

"Hello? Hello?"

"Okay," she said. "But let me ask."

"Well?"

"Daddy said it's okay. I'll see you Saturday, Maggie Hammond."

"You too, Cheryl Hardiman."

When I hung up, Mama and Mary walked into the house. "Why aren't you cleaned up?" Mama asked.

"Well, the boys beat me to the bathroom. Edward is in there now."

. . . .

"Maggie, you've been smilin' ever since you've got home" Mary said. "Somethings up." She gave me a curious look.

I tried to reassure her with a pinky swear that nothing was up, but all the while inside, I couldn't wait until Saturday.

The rest of the week was the same, Aunt Pearl babysat Lewis while Aunt Louise came to the orchard with us. Instead of picking one tree, our family picked two. The boys worked on one tree, and if they finished, they helped me, Mama, Aunt Louise, and Mary.

Mama and Aunt Louise yelled, "Okay, everyone. Lunch time."

I was startled and tired. I loosened my hand from the bucket of cherries.

"Edward, be careful coming down that ladder," Aunt Louise said. "Your little brother is walking under it."

Mama and Aunt Louise sat on the blanket under the cherry tree next to where they picked from. The boys walked two trees away, but in Mama's eyesight.

I spread the other blanket on the ground near Mama and Aunt Louise. "Come on, Mary and Joe," I said. "You two can sit here with me." I set the two cherry buckets and crates next to us.

"I don't want to sit on that nasty bucket," Mary grumbled.

"That's all right," I said. "You can sit on the blanket. I set them there just in case you did."

We ate sandwiches and some cherries, drank strawberry Kool-aid, and had pound cake for dessert. The boys were laying on their backs, arms underneath their heads. Joe stood up and leaned against the tree to stretch his legs. Mary squinted. "Maggie, is that ..." She paused.

I used my hand to block the sun. "Mama, it's Aunt Pearl with Janet, Missionary White's granddaughter, and her mother. You know them from the church?"

"Stop teasing," Edward said. "Why would they come here?"

"No. Look!" I said.

Mike and Edward got up from the blanket.

Mama and Aunt Louise didn't look surprised. "Mama," I asked, "did you know they were coming?"

Mama nodded. She moved closer to me. "I hope you're not embarrassed."

"I never thought Janet would be here. We talked about her coming on Saturday, not today."

"Maggie," Mama said. "That wasn't my intent. Her mother asked because she hasn't seen anyone pick cherries. They've seen cotton pickin' and wondered if it was the same."

"Where is Lewis? I thought Aunt Pearl was watching him?"

"Miss Ollie's watching him."

Janet walked briskly over the tall grass and called out my name.

"What are you doing here?" I asked.

"It's boring at home, so I asked to come."

"Well, let me show you around my place of employment. Do you want to try and pick some cherries?"

"Sure. This seems a lot different than being in the heat pickin' cotton."

"Oh, believe me, we work the black muck fields, in direct sunlight, topping onions. But we have shears. They look like oversized scissors."

I walked over to Mama. "This isn't that bad. I'd feel far worse explaining welfare."

During the short time that Janet was at the orchard, I showed her the rows of cherries, and for once, our conversation wasn't about junior high school or the different ways to play hopscotch.

I explained, "We fill our buckets, dump the cherries into crates, and Mama and Aunt Louise count them. At the end of the day, we're paid for the cherries we've picked."

Janet stumbled, trying to keep up. "These weeds are taller than across the road where you guys play baseball."

"That's all right" I said.

"Sorry. I thought you hadn't noticed."

"Just step higher and push down."

Janet walked in between me and Mary. She reached her long arms around the both of us. "Although it's been a short visit this summer, I'm really gonna miss you, Maggie," Janet said. She looked at Mary and squeezed her shoulder, "You two, squirt."

"Girls!"

Mama waved for us to catch up. We ran to the next tree.

Aunt Pearl called Janet over and told her it was time to go. Mary and I waved until we couldn't see them.

The boys and Aunt Louise were on the last tree. Mary, Mama, and I bent over and picked up our cherry buckets. I noticed Mama grab her lower back.

"Are you all right, Mama?" I asked.

"I'm fine. Let's finish this last tree."

Mama always says that she's fine.

I was so happy we were done picking. We just needed to wait for Mr. Gill's final tally.

. . . .

We share a driveway with Uncle Ted and Aunt Louise. When we got home, Tuffy was sitting on the top step, probably waiting for his dinner. No one rushed out of the car today. Everyone was tired from picking in the orchard. She straightened the rearview mirror so that the boys, who sat in the back seat, saw her eyes.

"The girls can get in the bath first. Do you boys hear me?"

One brother pushed the front seat. Sighs came from the others.

"You boys have a choice to wait or go to Aunt Louise's. You can do what you do most times: share the hose or tub outside."

Silence.

"The reason why the girls use the bathroom first is because there are only two of them. There are four of you. And you boys know you're not gonna bathe together. I hope this will settle any arguments."

Mary was in the tub when the telephone rang. It was Cheryl. We talked about Saturday and Janet coming over. When I went back into the bathroom, Mary slapped the water.

"What's wrong?" I asked.

"Why didn't you let me know that Janet was coming over? What's the big secret?"

"It wasn't necessarily a big secret, but Mama wanted you to hang out with her after choir practice and go to town."

Mary looked at me as though she didn't believe me.

"I'm not lying." I said. "You can ask her."

She sighed.

Mama called all of us into the living room. "There are still some clothes on the clothesline. Each of you can grab a handful, especially the clothes on the ground and the ones with no clothespins."

Mary and I brought ours into the house. We went to the bedroom to fold them. I heard the clinking sound of pots and pans from the kitchen. I decided to talk to Mama about tomorrow and Mary.

"I'll be right back, Mary," I said.

When I got to the kitchen, there was Mama on her knees, nearly half her body inside a the lower cupboard, looking for what seemed like a certain pot because the others were scattered on the floor. Although I wanted to talk about Mary, I played it off by pouring a glass of Kool-Aid to ease into the question.

"Hey, Mama. Getting ready to cook something?"

"No," she answered. "I'm tired of not being able to find the pots and pans I want, so I'm rearranging them."

"Um, Mama, do you remember when I spoke to you about Cheryl and Janet coming over to visit, and you said you'd watch Mary?"

"Yes."

"Well, Cheryl and I voted?"

"What?" Mama had a face full of wrinkles. "Voted."

"Yes," I said. "We voted and decided that it's all right if she hangs with us tomorrow."

"Are you sure? You can't change your minds."

I looked into the front living room to make sure Mary hadn't listened. "This summer, Mama, Mary has gotten attached to Cheryl and me. Besides, who else does she have to hang out with?"

"Okay," Mama said. She wiggled her pointer finger at me with those Mama eyes. "But don't come to me with one complaint."

140

Dear Diary,

Seems like a new beginning. Mary will hang around with me and my friends. I don't want her to grow up too soon.

Chapter 26

To New Beginnings

Saturday on the front porch, I stood next to the oversized chair. I leaned against the window, waiting for Cheryl and Janet to arrive. I wondered about how they would behave with each other. Would they argue and fuss? Then I remembered what Mama told us to do when something bothered us: pray. I leaned against the window, hands clasped together, rested my chin against them, and prayed.

Fifteen minutes later, right on time, Cheryl's father pulled their car into our driveway.

"Mama! Mama!" I hollered.

"What's wrong?" Mama hurried to the front porch, a concerned look on her face.

"Cheryl's here."

As I ran to the back door, Mama hollered, "Maggie, stop running through the house."

I bumped into Mary, almost knocking her down. "Sorry

Mary."

"Where's the fire?" she asked.

Cheryl's father had barely stopped the car when Cheryl opened the door. Her father hollered at her. You would have thought we hardly ever saw each other.

Mr. Hardiman, Cheryl's father, walked to the house. "How you doin', Mrs. Hammond?"

"Blessed. And you?"

"I'm blessed, too."

Edward and Cousin William were in the yard playing catch. "What's the big deal?" Edward asked. "They act like they haven't seen each other before."

"I heard that, Edward," Mama said. "Be nice. And you and your cousin better stay out of those back woods. I don't want you smellin' like skunks or pickin' up snakes and puttin' them in your pockets." She pointed her finger.

Just as we were about to go in the house, Mary noticed Janet and her mother coming down the driveway.

"Look," she said. "Here come Janet."

Cheryl and I both stopped and turned around. Janet didn't look happy to see Cheryl. She hugged me, but not Cheryl. Silently,

I prayed, *Please, God, let this visit go smoothly. Well, as smoothly as possible, meaning no fights. Thank you.*

Mr. Hardiman let Mama know that he had to run an errand and would be back to pick up Cheryl. Mother White followed Mama inside the house for a glass of Mama's fresh-squeezed lemonade. Cheryl, Janet, Mary, and I sat on the front porch. Strategically, I sat in the oversized chair with Janet. Cheryl's face showed her displeasure. She sat on the other cushion, next to me and by the door. Mary sat on another set of pillow cushions, in between Cheryl and Janet.

I thought about talking about Janet surprising our family at the cherry orchard, but decided against it. I didn't feel that would set well with Cheryl. I didn't want her to think we had invited her. Instead, I silently, prayed for something to break up the awkwardness.

"Pop fly!" Mike yelled.

Mike had gone across the road to play baseball. We stood up and looked.

I hollered, "Run, Mike! Run!"

"Do you guys want to watch the boys play baseball instead of writing in our dairies?" I asked.

"That sounds good to me," Cheryl said.

Cheryl and I smiled.

"How about you, Janet?"

"Okay," Janet answered.

One of the boys next door came up to bat. Janet looked his way. He tapped his bat on the cardboard twice, raised the bat, and smack. It was a line drive straight to Mike, but Mike didn't catch it. Janet jumped up and down and smiled. It was the first smile I had seen since we were together.

"Do you like the neighbor boy?" I whispered to Janet. "You know he's older? And you *do* know that you're only here for the summer. . ."

"Please don't remind me," she said.

We watched a few more boys bat. Then Cheryl and Mary asked if we were going to write in our diaries.

We began to walk back to the front porch. "Wait a minute," Cheryl said. "Let's walk up the road a little bit instead."

The four of us walked side by side, unless a car drove by. We kicked rocks, talking about boys and other things. I had to remind everyone, " My little sister is with us, and she might not want to hear about bras and how large our busts are."

"Yes, I do," Mary said.

"Okay," I said. "But you better not tell Mama."

We changed the topic and talked about junior high. Again. We decided that maybe it wouldn't be so bad.

"How about you, Janet?" Cheryl asked. "What will it be like for you down south? You've heard our crying about it."

I looked at Janet, not sure how she would respond to Cheryl's question.

Janet stopped and told us, "Down south, we have other things to be concerned about besides boys and popularity. We have the problem of the whites not liking the coloreds and what side of the hall you can and can't walk down."

"I'm sorry," Cheryl said.

"But you guys live outside of town. How does that make you feel?" Janet asked.

"It seems the same, but they're not as mean-spirited."

While listening to Janet, I began to think of her situation down south and ours up north. I began to feel less nervous about going into junior high.

"You guys," I said, "maybe it won't be the end of the world. Once we walk through the doors."

"Maybe not." Cheryl uncrossed her arms.

We had stopped on the road. A car honked. We walked over to Aunt Louise's house and sat on the wooden swings.

"You aren't scared of the girls," Mary asked.

"It's not all of the girls," Cheryl said, "Just a few of them."

"Where I live," Janet said, "none of the girls are friendly to the coloreds. It doesn't matter if you are popular or not. You just walk into the school like you belong."

"But the control areas are the bathroom and lunch tables."

Mary asked if we could play hopscotch before Janet and Cheryl left.

Mama leaned out the door, "Janet, your mother is ready to go."

We hugged each other and waved. As Janet was leaving, she rolled down the car window and hollered, "See you tomorrow at church. . . The White Cloud Church of God In Christ."

Mary and I waved back. "See you tomorrow."

Seems like my prayers were answered, I thought.

. . . .

It's Sunday morning, and once again, we lined our cars up like we were in a parade: Uncle Ted's car at the mouth of the driveway, and Mama's car behind Uncle Ted's, waiting for Uncle John to slowly pull up and park along the road in front of our house.

Mama asked Uncle Ted to wait a minute for Thomas. He was in the bathroom. It was so hot that Mama let us wait under the weeping willow tree, but we had to make sure not to get dirty.

When Thomas ran out of the house, he was his usual self on Sunday, complaining about church. "No one should have to sit inside a church in those hot choir robes in this heat," Thomas moaned.

"As much as you've been going to church, you should be used to it," I replied.

"Shut up, Maggie!"

"No. You shut up!"

"Okay. Okay," Mama said. "You two simmer down. This is God's day."

Aunt Louise walked out of her house, letting the screen door slam. As she passed by our car, she said, "And we'll do as we've always done on Sundays: GO TO CHURCH."

"Sorry, Aunt Louise," Thomas said.

After Thomas got in the back seat of the car, Uncle Ted left the driveway. Uncle John's car was last.

When the church service ended, dinner wasn't served. That didn't stop Cheryl from meeting me at the apple tree.

"Maggie." Janet frowned. "Must we climb that tree?"

"What's wrong with climbing trees? You've done this before with us."

"But I don't want to climb trees all the time and mess up my dress."

"We won't climb the tree that long today anyway because we're having dinner at home. I want to see if we can all visit again soon this week because this is your last week, right?"

Janet didn't look happy. I thought my plans this summer had worked. At least, Janet acted like they had. The four of us, Cheryl, Mary, Janet and I had formed a friendship, or so I thought.

"Cheryl," I said. "Maggie and I need to leave early today. We're going to eat at my Aunt Louise's house."

"Maggie! Mary!"

We turned around. Mama and Aunt Pearl were calling for us.

"Talk to y'all later," I said. "Come on , Mary. We don't want to be late."

Mary walked faster than me, arms flailing back and forth. Janet's attitude toward Cheryl caught me off guard. I couldn't figure out what was wrong, and that bothered me.

Mary didn't say a word.

"Why are you so quiet?" I asked. Please tell me right now what's wrong."

"We don't want to miss time with the family now, do we?"

I couldn't help but think that it was just last Saturday when Janet gave us tips on how to handle the popular girls in junior high. We laughed and didn't mind that we all were together. Today, Janet walked ahead of me, stomping on the rocks that paved the church's driveway.

Most times, my sister and I rode in our car to and from church. Mike and Edward took turns riding with either Uncle John or Uncle Ted. We loved to ride in different cars because that gave us more room to sit.

I watched Cheryl climb over her fence, while Mama drove out of the church's driveway.

Janet's family was invited to break bread with our family.

"Break bread" is when a visitor or church member has dinner with another church member's family. Thank God it was a sunny day. We set up two card tables, under the weeping willow tree, all the while shooing Tuffy away.

Janet wasn't cordial at the dinner table. I tried to play it off, but Mama, Aunt Louise, and Aunt Pearl noticed.

Mama pulled me aside, asking me to help bring out more silverware from the house. "Maggie, isn't this Janet's last week here?"

"Yes."

"Do you girls have any plans?" Mama asked. "You're always writing something in those diaries of yours."

"Mama, you read my diary?"

"No. I was putting it away laundry and noticed it sitting on top of your dresser."

Darn it, I thought. Then I answered, "Ah. We don't have any special plans, Mama. I mean, we haven't decided yet."

Then I heard Janet's voice. "Wow, these potatoes taste good. And the cornbread, like down south."

"Well," Mama said, "our family came from down south, from Natchez, to be exact."

"All of you?" Janet's mother asked.

"Yes," Aunt Louise said.

We gave Tuffy the bones from the leftovers. He ran under the tree, gnawing on them. The kids, even Janet, were given clean-up responsibilities. I helped put the food away, wrapping the bowl of potatoes, and the fried chicken, and slid the jar of Kool-Aid into our refrigerator. Janet and Mary folded the plastic tablecloths after wiping them clean.

"Mama, I did my part to clean up," I said. "Can I go now?"

"As long as you have finished what you were supposed to do. Maybe take Janet and Mary with you."

When I got home, I took off my apron and put it in the bathroom hamper. Then I called Cheryl.

"Is Janet coming over?"

"I don't know," I said. "You two acted so funny today."

"Yes, I noticed," Cheryl said.

"What's wrong? Over the past week, I thought all of us were getting along."

"I'm not sure. But I still want to surprise Janet with a cake."

"Are you sure you know how to make one?"

"Mama said she'd help me with the directions. We can sit under the apple tree by our church."

"And Janet won't mind?"

"Don't worry. I'll talk to her." I put my hand over the phone. "Be quiet. I can't hear on the phone. Cheryl, I have to go. Mary's calling for me."

"Okay. See you Saturday."

• • • •

During lunch, Mary and I walked through the cherry orchard and ate our sandwiches. For some reason, the day felt different. Somehow the day felt different. When we got home, we did our usual activities: cleaning up and then sitting on the front porch with our diaries. Mary walked toward the porch but stopped. She stood in the doorway, her diary in hand.

"Well, are you gonna sit down or stand there?" I asked.

Mary looked down at me. "Are you sure you want me to sit in the oversized chair? Last time, Janet sat there."

I scooted over, patted my hand on the cushion, and didn't say anything but smiled. Mary opened her diary, flipped the pages, and began to write.

"Cheryl has invited us over to sit under the apple tree tomorrow. You know, just to hang out," I said. "Do you want to go?"

Mary didn't answer, but she began to write in her diary. She held one side up so that I couldn't see what she was writing.

"Is there something wrong?" I asked her.

Mary pushed the rug back and forth with her feet. "This summer, I have gotten to know Cheryl better, and I know she's your best friend, but-"

"But what?" I asked.

"Every day, after we got back from the fields, I enjoyed being with you," Mary said, giving me a bashful look. "Why can't we . . . never mind. I'll go tomorrow."

"You sure?"

"Yes. I'm sure."

"Good. Aunt Louise will take us over to Cheryl's house at 11:30. Mama has to work."

The next day, the sun beamed from the sky. There was no breeze. Mary and I both washed up and waited for Aunt Louise. As we stared out the back porch windows, Tuffy chased a squirrel around the tree. The squirrel won as it scurried up the weeping willow tree.

"Where's Aunt Louise?" Mary asked.

"I don't know. Usually she's honking the horn."

"Could you go and get her?" Mary asked. "We should have left by now."

"Why are you in such a hurry?"

"Well, I didn't want to tell you this, but I'm excited too. You and Cheryl are the ones who hang out, but this summer, you have included me."

"I love you, Mary, and so does Cheryl." I gave her a big hug. "Now, let me call Aunt Louise."

The phone rang two times before Uncle Ted answered. "Is everything all right?" I asked. "Will Aunt Louise be able to take us over to my friend Cheryl's house next to the church?"

"Last I knew, Maggie, she was laying down in our room. She said that she had a headache."

When I hung up the phone, Mary sensed my frustration. "What's wrong?"

"We can't leave yet. Aunt Louise has a headache."

Soon, Uncle Ted called back. "Come on over. I have to be at the church anyway to help clean up."

I sat in the back of the car, and Mary sat in the front. Uncle Ted slowly drove into the back parking lot by the church's kitchen and the apple tree. Brother White, Janet's grandfather, was already in the back of the church. He, Uncle Ted, and Uncle John were the janitors at church.

Good, I thought. The picnic table was under the apple tree, but not Cheryl. It was 12:15.

"Go knock on the door and make sure she's home," Uncle Ted said.

I hopped over the fence and knocked on the door. "Cheryl, why aren't you at the picnic table?" I asked.

"The cake," she said.

"What about the cake?"

"Well. . ."

"I bet it'll taste real good," I said.

"This is the worse cake I have ever seen," Cheryl said. "It's lopsided."

"What's the cake for?" Janet asked. "Is there something happening at church?"

Cheryl spread an old sheet over the picnic table and moved the cake to the center of the table.

"Janet, I wanted to say thank you for being a friend to me this summer," Cheryl said. "Even when you thought I had taken your friend away. After tomorrow, I won't see you until next year, so I baked this cake for you. Actually, it's from all of us."

Janet's eyes began to water. She looked at each of us and tried to hold back tears.

"You girls have a good time," Uncle Ted said. "I'll check on you later."

"Don't worry, Ted. I'll keep an eye on them too while I do my laundry," Cheryl's mama said.

"I'll also be around, working on the church property," Brother White said.

"Janet, you can have the first slice," Maggie said.

"Why don't we all take a bite from this slice?" Janet said. "It can unify us."

"Hey," Mary said. "It doesn't taste bad."

"You're right," Janet said. "It doesn't look good, but it tastes pretty good."

The cake party was going better than I thought it would. But, we decided to go sit and talk under the apple tree. It was too hot to hop, jump, or run. Cheryl's Mama brought over their tic-tac-toe board. Cheryl's brother annoyed us, begging for cake. To make him leave, we gave him a slice.

Brother White leaned out of the church's kitchen door. "I'm getting ready to leave, girls. Janet, your mother will pick you up later."

"What will you remember from this summer?" Cheryl asked Janet.

"That I stayed without getting homesick," she said. "And. . . getting to know you girls."

"What about you, Cheryl?" Janet asked.

Cheryl smiled and her dimples showed. "Getting to know you, and the fact that you ate our cake."

"I'll remember the suggestions you gave us for junior high school," I said. "What about you, sis?"

"You girls!" Mary said.

Cheryl's mama held a basket of clothes that she had taken of the clothesline. "Cheryl, it's time to come home," she said.

Cheryl's dog met her at the fence. Next, Janet's mama drove into the church parking lot and got out of the car. Janet ran toward their car.

"Did you girls have a good time?" Janet's mama asked.

"Yes," Janet said with cake in hand. "As you see, they made me a cake. It tasted good."

When Janet's mother drove out of the parking lot, Janet leaned out the window and waved. "Cheryl, Maggie, and Mary," she yelled. "I hope to see you again!"

Dear Diary,

I made a new friend, named Janet, from down south. During the summer, she attended our church a lot, and we'd sit under the apple tree. I'll remember what she told me and Cheryl about our fears of entering junior high. She said to please not wear those braids. I will never forget all four of us writing in our diaries and sitting in the oversized chair on our front porch.

Chapter 27

6th Grade

School started Tuesday, after Labor Day. On the refrigerator, Mama had taped our list of chores for the week, this time with the bus watch assignments. The list had the days of the week with our names: Mike, Edward, Thomas, me, and the twins.

Since Mama had taken a fill-in job at the Fremont nursing facility, Mike had to make sure everyone was up, dressed for school, and lined up single file for our bus.

"Thomas," Mike yelled from the bathroom, "hurry up. It's your turn to watch for the bus."

There were two dressers with mirrors in our room. One with Mama's clothes and the other her vanity. I sat thinking of Janet, and remembering what she said to Cheryl and me: "Don't have so many braids. Try to wear a ponytail."

I picked up the comb, parted one row of my hair, and made a French braid along the front of my head. I tucked the end of the braid and put a bobby pin underneath to make sure it wouldn't come loose. The rest of my hair I brushed into a ponytail. I used more bobby pins to keep loose hair in the back tucked underneath.

While looking in the mirror, I noticed Mama's pink can of Aqua Net hairspray on the corner of her dresser. "Mary," I said. "You see that big pink can over there, on Mama's dresser?"

"Yes."

"Could you hand it to me?"

She brought it to me. I read the back of the can. "The Aqua Net line of professional hairspray products provide all day, all-weather hold throughout all weather conditions."

"Is that what you want for your hair?" Mary asked.

"Yep," I said. "All day hold."

The cap top was hard to pull off. I squeezed the top until it slipped from my hand. "Stand back," I told Mary. "I don't want any to get into your eyes."

I took the bobby pins out from the back of my hair and sprayed in a circle motion, coughing in between each spray. I stopped and touched my head, making sure no strands stuck out. Just in case the spray didn't do what it said, I replaced the bobby pins.

Mary stood and watched. "Maggie," she said. "Your hair

looks great."

"Thank you, Mary. Do you want me to brush yours?"

Mary sat in the chair. I brushed her hair and placed a black headband in the front.

"What do you think?" I asked.

"It's beautiful," Mary said.

We walked out of the bedroom. Thomas sat at the dining room table, bent over. He put on one shoe, stretched his arms over his head, and then bent over to the same shoe.

"Was it that tiring to put on one shoe?" I asked.

He didn't answer.

Thomas was a year younger than me, in fifth grade. Except for when he occasionally he tried to trick me, he was a good brother. Just lazy. Mama felt that he was too irresponsible to watch for the bus last year, but all that had changed now.

"Mike!" I whined. "Thomas is taking too long, and I have to wipe the table clean."

"I have two feet, and therefore, I have two shoes to put on and tie up."

Mike came out of the boy's bedroom. He pushed the curtain back from the doorway. "Hurry up, Thomas," he said as he walked past him and into the bathroom.

Thomas walked to the porch, but not without grumbling.

"There is a list on the refrigerator door for everything: cleaning the kitchen, sweeping and mopping the floors, taking the garbage out, dusting, mowing the lawn, feeding the pigs and chickens. There's a list for-"

"Thomas, please just go watch for the bus," Mike said loudly. "Everyone has a chore on the list, and today, this is yours."

As Thomas walked past me, I said, "I believe you don't like to watch for the bus because that means you'll have to get up earlier for school."

He continued to walk past me. I spoke louder. "We all know that you love to sleep in and are always the last one to get up."

Thomas flicked his hand toward me.

"That's why I've given all of you nicknames."

Thomas stopped. He turned around. "What?"

"I don't know if I want to say," I said in a sassy voice.

He walked to the front porch. "That's all right."

"The lazy one," I blurted. "That's your nickname."

I had given everyone but the twins nicknames. Mike was "head of the house." Edward was "the militant one" because he always debated.

Thomas was finally on the front porch. I followed him, opening the door he tried to close. "Mary?" I said, surprised. "You're supposed to be in the bedroom, putting on your socks and shoes, not sitting in the oversized chair."

"I can't stay and listen?" Mary asked.

To me, Mary always seemed older than her age. She watched and listened to everything us older kids did. Joe, on the other hand, loved to follow the boys and to get under their skin, so to speak. He wanted to play basketball, baseball and Mike riding him on his bike.

"Don't worry, Mary," I said. "You and Joe will be able to watch for the bus in a few years."

The twins would have to be in fifth grade before Mama would let them watch for the bus.

I walked into the kitchen and lined all the lunches on the dining room table. Our names were marked on each bag.

I maneuvered my body to see Thomas. "Have you seen the bus yet?" I asked in a concerned tone.

Sarcastically, he answered. "Yeah. There's no bus."

"Mary and Joe," Mike said. "Come sit on the sofa. I don't

want to have to find you when it's time to line up for the bus."

Mike made sure all the lights were off except for the lamp in the living room. I sat in front of the mirror again to make sure no strands of hair stuck out.

"The bus is coming up the road next to Ole' Man Garrison's house!" He yelled. He hurried us out of the house, shut the door behind him, and scolded Thomas for not letting us know sooner.

Mr. Hucklebee drove our route last year and bus 10. It had a flat front. We named it pug nose. Mr. Hucklebee honked the horn twice as he stopped in front of our house. We rushed to line up. The Harris boys, their sister, and Lewis rushed to stand behind us.

Mr. Hucklebee had a rule that if we weren't in line by the time he closed the doors, we were left. Once or twice, this had happened to Mike and Lewis. If they couldn't get Aunt Pearl to take them to school, they'd walk. I know for a fact that Mike would rather walk than call our Mama or Aunt Pearl. There wasn't enough explaining in the world. Walking was a better choice.

The doors opened. "Welcome to a new school year, kids," Mr. Williams said. "Sit in any empty seat."

Mike moved to the front of the line to help the twins find a seat. He paused. There were no empty seats in the front. Since the twins were too young to sit by themselves, Mike sat with Joe. "Maggie, you sit with Mary," he said.

"Mike, why is that the coloreds always have to sit near or in the back of the bus, scattered with just enough whites among us so that we don't complain?"

"Turn around, Maggie," Mike said. "I'll tell Mama later."

"Maggie?" Mary said. "Can't we open the windows? There's no air."

I made a fan from notebook paper and fanned Mary. "Is that better?"

"No," she said.

I grabbed the seat in front of me for balance and stood. "Mr. Hucklebee!"

He made eye contact with me. "You have to sit down while the bus is moving."

"Could we open some windows?" I asked. "It's hotter inside than outside."

Again, he made eye contact. His lips tightened together. "You can pull it halfway, but don't stick your arms or head out the windows."

Mr. Hucklebee kept his eyes on the road but also noticed

who opened their windows.

The bus turned toward the elementary school. Mike helped Mary and Joe get off the bus and to their classes. From there he walked down the hill to the high school.

Mr. Hucklebee closed the bus door. I began to get nervous and hoped I would remember everything that Janet had told Cheryl and me about junior high.

I stood and waited to get off the bus. I smoothed down my hair and made sure my clothes were all right.

One thing Janet had told us was that our wardrobe decision was crucial. Although I wanted to wear my pink pedal pushers with a white short-sleeve top, I couldn't. The school system was smarter than me and had mailed out the dress code to our parents.

The boys could wear long pants, but no shorts. The girls had to wear dresses or a skirt and top, but no pants or shorts.

"Good luck today," Mr. Hucklebee told me. "You'll probably need it."

"Thanks, Mr. Hucklebee." I frowned.

Cheryl and Jackie waited in front of the main doors of the school.

"Hey!" I hollered. "Where's Sarah?"

"Here I am." She hollered back. "Can't start junior high without me."

"I see everyone got the memo on how to dress," I said.

"And don't forget the hair." Cheryl patted her curls.

Jackie's hair was brushed back into a ponytail. Sarah had a lot of hair, and it was long. She had one long French braid down the middle of her head with a rubber band at the end.

"Did everyone get the letter about the school meeting in the gym?" Cheryl asked.

We nodded.

"How was your bus ride?" I asked.

"Back of the bus," Cheryl said sarcastically.

"Doesn't that bother you?" I asked.

"Hell, yeah," Cheryl said.

"That doesn't mean it's the school's fault," Jackie said. "Maybe it's the way the kids are picked up and that most of the seats happen to be in the back."

"How would you know?" I asked. "You're not riding the bus this year."

"Look at the positive." Jackie said. "At least you don't have to walk seven miles."

She was always the optimistic one of the group.

Ring. Ring.

"Which bell was that?" Cheryl asked.

Kids pushed us aside and hurried down the hallway to the gym for the school meeting.

"I guess that was the last bell," Jackie said.

"Please stop running!" the teacher's hollered at the kids.

In the gym, everyone sat with their class. The junior high students sat on the bleachers. The room buzzed with kids talking.

Bam! Bam! Bam!

The room quickly came to order. I turned toward the stage.

"Hello, White Cloud junior high and high school students. As most of you know, I'm Principal Jackson."

The gym door opened. John, the class clown, walked in. The principal' eyes followed John to the junior high class group. He watched John stumble over the boys and girls until he sat down. Everyone else watched.

"The entire school is glad that you could make it, Mr. Smith," the principal said. "Now, do you mind if I continue? Oh, and please see me in my office immediately after the assembly."

"Nothing's gonna happen," I said. "His father is the mayor."

The principal gave a welcome back to school speech and introduced the office staff and teachers, who sat two rows behind him on the stage. As he called their names, they stood up, smiled, and sat back down.

The principal said, "Before everyone hurries out of here, please wait for a teacher to lead you out of the door. From there, you can go to your lockers and class."

The seniors were dismissed first. The rest of the classes followed. The sixth-grade class waited. The upper classmen crowded the doorway.

Someone threw a wad of paper over our heads. It landed two rows in front of me. When I turned around, there was Susan Miller: one of the most popular girls in the fifth grade.

I nudged Cheryl. "There's Miss Everything, Susan Miller."

"Where?" she asked.

"Sitting near the top row, next to the girl in the blue blouse with the white ribbon in her hair."

Cheryl didn't give her any attention. She turned around and reminded me of what Janet had told us about the popular girls.

Bam! Bam! The principle spoke loudly into the microphone. "Eighth, seventh, and sixth graders, please follow your teachers."

The maintenance men folding chairs and the sixth graders' voices echoed in the gym.

"Class?" Mr. Robinson stood tall and repeated himself. "That includes you, Mr. Upright."

Since White Cloud is a small town, everyone knew everyone. It wasn't surprising that Mr. Robinson had to call out Jonathan Upright. He sat next to Susan, in the popular group.

"As I was saying, in the letters sent to your homes this summer, your class schedule was attached."

Kids located their letters and read them.

"If your first period class is English, please get behind me. If you are in math, line up behind Ms. Kraft."

Kids began to run down the bleachers like there was a fire until Mr. Robinson yelled, "Everyone, stop right where you are."

Susan looked at me. She leaned over and whispered something into her friend's ear. They both snickered.

Mr. Robinson continued. "The top row can walk down. The next row, and so on. Please go directly to your classes."

The hallways were crowded. Kids bumped into each other or stopped to talk at their lockers. A football was tossed over our heads. Someone yelled, "Look Out!"

"I guess this is part of being in the high school building," Cheryl yelled to me and Jackie. Susan was near the end of the math teacher's line.

"I love it," Jackie said.

"We need to keep up with our class," I said to my friends. "Walk faster. I can't get a tardy on the first day of school."

I thought about last night. Mama had called us to the dining room table and had given us her going back to school speech. "I don't want to have any tardy notes from your teachers," she said. "No fights. And by no means can any of you change classes."

The part about changing classes was directed at Mike since he was the only one in high school and could select classes.

"Your mama gave y'all that going back to school sermon, didn't she?" Cheryl asked.

Fifth grade was so much easier with no lockers or locker combinations to remember or books to carry. Books were kept inside desks. But one of the things I missed most was going into the woods before classes to make our houses. We had done that since first grade. Making houses in between the trees from branches and leaves wasn't something you did in junior high.

. . . .

At the dinner table, Mike and I made eye contact. I nodded my head toward Mama and mouthed for him to tell Mama about the bus seats.

Mike took a sip of his Kool-Aid and set his glass down. "Mama?" He looked toward me. "This year on the bus ... the seats are the same as last year. The colored sit in back of the bus."

"All of you?" Mama asked.

"Except for a few."

"Where do they sit?"

"Near the back," I interrupted.

"Tomorrow, I'll be home when you get on the bus," Mama said. "And I'll see for myself." She looked around the table. "Let's finish dinner."

The next day, my alarm rang earlier. It was my turn to watch for the bus. Not wanting to wake Mary, I quietly slid the hangers along the closet rail and walked into the bathroom.

I was concerned about my blouse. I stood in front of the mirror and tugged with both hands to button up my blouse. All the buttons slid into the button holes, except by my breasts. A gap from the buttons formed there.

When I came out of the bathroom, Mama was in the kitchen, making breakfast. "Mama?" I whined. "Can you help me fix this gap with my blouse?"

After she turned off the grits, I followed her into the bedroom. On her dresser, she got the circular tin canister that held the safety pins.

"Stand still so that I don't poke you," she said. "Now, let's see how this looks."

"The blouse is just too small."

Mama went to the other side of the bedroom. She pushed the curtain back in the closet that we shared.

Mary had awakened and sat up in bed to watch us. "What are you looking for?" she asked.

"What you guys looking for?" Mary asked.

"I'm trying to find a blouse for your sister that fits," Mama said. "Since you're awake, go and see if your brothers are in the bathroom. If not, you can get cleaned up for school."

Mama slid the hangers along the metal rail and said, "Here's one of my blouses. Try this one on."

It was a white blouse with buttons down the back. Mama

stood behind me, tugged, pulled the blouse toward the middle of my back, and tucked it inside my skirt.

"Now, turn around and look in the mirror," she said.

Slowly, I turned around. The blouse didn't fit perfectly, but it was better than what I was going to wear. All I had to do was fold up the sleeves.

Mama said, "I've noticed you walk a little hunched over the past few weeks, with your arms folded. You're growing up so fast," she said. "I'll look in my pile of material pieces and see what I have to fix your blouses. Since you don't have an older sister for hand-me-downs, I'll also talk to the social worker today and see if she can find some blouses that would fit you."

"Thanks, Mama," I said. But I was thinking, *How is this gonna help me in gym class today?*

Dear Diary,

Same problem as yesterday. My breasts are growin' faster and faster, it seems. Mama had me try on one of her blouses.

Chapter 28

You Tell Me

When bus 10 passed Miss Ollie's house, I poked my head into the living room and hollered, "The bus is going toward Diamond Lake."

Thomas sat in the dining room, eating his grits.

"Did you hear that, Thomas?"

He tapped his spoon against his bowl and didn't answer me.

Mary walked out to help watch for the bus. "I see the Harris family already waiting."

"I guess they don't want to miss the bus," I said. "Remember yesterday? They had to run to get in line."

Mary rested her arms against the window that faced Aunt Pearl's house, anxious to call for the bus.

"Mary?" I said. "You see the bus coming down the road next to the Garrison's field?"

I don't think she saw it at first. The trees were tall and full of leaves. "You see it yet?"

She jumped with excitement. "There! It's turning down our road!" she hollered. "Everyone should get in line."

This is where Thomas was supposed to train getting everyone on the bus. Instead, he ran with Mike, Edward, and Joe to the door, grabbing their lunches from the table in the dining room. Mama leaned out the front door and waved as the bus driver drove away, not before noticing some of the seat arrangements.

I met Cheryl, Jackie, and Sarah by my locker. The first two weeks, we waited as long as we could for the bathroom because we didn't want to run into Susan and her group. It was enough drama to fight for the mirror with the upper classmen.

"Come on, let's hurry," I said.

The bathroom wasn't crowded yet, but we only had a few minutes.

"Watch my stall," I said.

While I used the bathroom, Sarah put on her mascara. Jackie brushed down her hair.

"Hurry Maggie," Cheryl said, "before the upper classmen come."

Cheryl used the bathroom after me, same stall.

The bathroom door opened. I faced the mirror. Jackie and

Sarah stood behind me.

"What are you guys doin' in here before us?" one of the upper classmen asked.

"I. . . we. . . I mean, we're leaving," I knocked on the stall for Cheryl.

She hurried out without washing her hands.

They laughed at her and pointed.

"Cheryl," I said. "Your skirt is caught inside your panties."

As we scurried out the door, it couldn't get any worse. We bumped into Susan and her group. "Watch where you're goin'."

"Whew." I rubbed my forehead. "That was close."

"I know," Cheryl said. "Thank God the upper classmen and Susan went to their lockers first."

"Isn't that what we're supposed to do?" Jackie asked.

"Yes," I said. "But if we had gone to our lockers, there is no way those girls would have let us into the bathroom. Then we would've been late for class."

At the end of third period, the bell rang. My most dreaded class was next. "Gym class," I moaned.

Gym was on the other side of the school. Cheryl and I rushed around kids in the crowded junior high hallway, which connected to the high school hallway. It was the only way to get to the gym before the bell rang.

When we walked through the doors, Mrs. Pollock, the gym teacher, glanced up at the clock on the wall and then back at us.

Mrs. Pollock shook her finger at me behind her office window. Our lockers were on the opposite side of her office window. Her lips formed the words, "Hurry up."

"I hate gym," I mumbled. "How do they expect me to wear this one-piece, ugly blue gym suit? It doesn't fit. And I'm sick of the boys staring at me every Friday when we have to dance."

I slammed my locker door and rushed to the gym. I found a spot in the back row for exercises.

The boys and girls shared the gym, but the teachers pulled a curtain across the middle of the gym to separate the classes.

Friday, during the second half of gym, the boys and girls danced together. The boys picked a girl. If the boys couldn't make up their minds, the teachers picked the girls for them. Some of the white boys would dance with to dance with a colored girl, some hesitantly.

I whispered to Cheryl, "Why do we have to dance? Our church doesn't allow it."

Mrs. Pollock blew her whistle. "Do I hear mumbling about dancing with the boys. This is not my rule but the school's. Today, you'll learn how to square dance."

I moved closer to Cheryl, who stood in front of me. "Who the hell wants to square dance?" she asked.

"Quiet, please," Mrs. Pollock commanded.

Mr. Loren, the boys' gym teacher, and Mrs. Pollock pushed the curtains aside. Kids began to scatter around the boy's half of the gym. Some boys and girls stood against the walls while others sat in the first row of the bleachers, talking and laughing.

"Everyone, be quiet!" Mr. Loren yelled. "It's time to pick your partners. Please form two lines across the middle of the gym. Girls, face the boys."

"Anthony, you can start," Mr. Loren said.

Anthony began to walk across the row. He stopped in the middle and stood in front of Megan.

"Luke, you pick next."

Luke walked up and down the row trying to decide who to dance with. He stopped in front of Karen.

After each boy picked a partner, Mr. Loren pointed toward the bleachers and asked them to sit in the first row. The girls who were not picked, which included Cheryl and me, moved closer to each other and formed a small line.

I hated all this picking and choosing. It was as if Cheryl and were the most unpopular girls in the gym. We stood there together with four other colored girls in the class.

"Cheryl, you knew none of us coloreds were gonna be picked," said.

"Do you think it's because of our skin color?" Cheryl asked.

I paused before answering. I felt as though some of it was because of our skin color. "Cheryl, look at who got picked first, compared to us not getting picked until last every time."

"What do you mean?"

Mr. Loren interrupted. "For those of you who seem to have a hard time choosing partners, Mrs. Pollock and I will choose for you."

Cheryl and I stood behind the rest of the girls who weren't picked.

"Maggie, you and Timothy are partners," Mrs. Pollock said.

"And John, you and Cheryl," Mr. Loren said.

John was skinny and shy, kept mostly to himself, and probably didn't dance. Timothy was my height, but overweight. In fifth grade, kids had teased Timothy and called him "Fatso." He'd watch the boys play baseball but was never picked to play on anyone's team.

Timothy stared at my shoes. His eyes then looked at my waist and paused at my breasts. I cleared my throat. He flinched as if I had startled him.

Kids sitting on the bleachers giggled. Some laughed. I gave them a sharp stare, which only made it worse. The kids pointed toward us.

Mr. Loren walked toward the bleachers. "Settle down. When you hear your name, please follow Mrs. Pollock. She will place you in a circle. The girls will stand inside the circle and the boys directly across from their partners."

Cheryl and I were in different circles.

"When the music starts, I want you to follow my instructions." Mr. Loren stood on the second row of the bleachers. "Can everyone hear me?"

"Yes," we answered.

I turned around, making eye contact with Cheryl. She didn't look excited either.

"Cheryl and Maggie?" Mrs. Pollock's piercing eyes were worse than Mama's. "Please pay attention."

Loud static came from the record player. No words. Just

music.

"Face your partners and bow," Mr. Loren said. "Now, join hands and circle to the left."

The music stopped.

"Everyone should be holding hands," Mr. Loren said. "I know this isn't the favorite part of gym class, but before you leave, you will learn how to square dance."

Mr. Loren resumed giving instructions. When the bell rang, we immediately dropped hands and ran into the locker rooms.

Cheryl and I had to shower and get to class quickly. I had to try my locker combination as fast as we could. I had to remember my combination twice before the door opened.

In a soft, concerned voice, Cheryl asked, "Are you going to take a shower today?"

"Who's checking the names?"

Cheryl walked to the end of the row of lockers and peeked her head around the last one. "Pam."

When Cheryl came back to our lockers, we looked into Mrs. Pollock's office, which was right in front of our lockers. She wasn't there.

"Wait here while I look inside the gym. Maybe she's there."

I noticed that she and Mr. Loren stood near the entrance of the boys' locker room, talking. If Cheryl and I were going to come up with a plan to avoid showering, this was our chance.

Every time I showered, the girls teased me, stared at my breasts, whispered, and giggled.

"You know what, Cheryl? If Mrs. Pollock questions us, we will come up with a story."

"You mean a lie?"

"Let's wipe off our sweat before Mrs. Pollock comes into her office," I said. "Ball your towel and toss it in the hamper with the damp ones before we leave."

"Maggie?"

"Please," I whimpered.

We tucked our blouses into our skirts and tied our shoes. Since I finished getting dressed first, I checked for Mrs. Pollock.

We ran out into the hallway before Mrs. Pollock returned.

"Oh no," I said. "I left my gym shoes on the floor. If I don't put them away, someone will steal them."

"What are you gonna do?" Cheryl asked.

"I'll catch up."

Cheryl's desk was in the row furthest from the classroom

door. She could see anyone who passed by.

I opened the door.

"Hello, Maggie. Glad you could join us."

"Sorry, Ms. Kraft," I said, thinking of what lie to tell. "I had to meet with Mrs. Pollock after gym class. It shouldn't happen again."

"Do you have a note from Mrs. Pollock?"

I pondered what to say. "I forgot," I said. "Can I bring it to class next time after gym?"

"For now, take a seat."

Ms. Kraft continued to write math problems on the chalkboard. Occasionally, she turned around to get our attention and quieted the idle whisperers.

Fifteen minutes later, the bell rang for the end of class and school. We began to shove papers inside our math books and rushed our desks to the door.

Ms. Kraft raised her arm and yelled, "Wait a minute, class. Your assignment is to review chapters four and five. Be ready for a quiz tomorrow."

"What do you think your mama's gonna do when she finds out you were late to class and lied about it?" Cheryl asked.

"Shh," I said. "This will be our secret. Don't tell Sarah or Jackie."

"Why not?" Cheryl asked.

"Just don't. Okay?"

Cheryl's locker was on the same side of the hall as mine but separated by the English classroom's doorway.

The hallway was filled with kids weaving in between each other. Jackie and Sarah waited for me at Cheryl's locker. Sarah covered her mouth and turned in my direction.

Cheryl and I kept secrets since early elementary school. She must had told Sarah and Jackie about gym class and not showering.

Raymond Grant, whose locker was across from Cheryl's, walked past me, laughing with his friends. I stood frozen in place. Dazed. I've had a crush on Raymond since fifth grade. He's very popular. He has an affluent colored family that lives on the outskirts of town in the rural area like ours, but they live in a big white house with a swimming pool. There were no goats, pigs, or chickens on their property.

"Maggie!"

I didn't answer right away.

"Maggie!"

Jackie waved and called my name. As I walked closer to Cheryl's locker I passed Raymond. I slowed down, hoping to smell his cologne. He always wore cologne.

"Come on," Sarah said.

"She's too interested in him." Cheryl nodded in Raymond's. "I betcha he doesn't take tardy notes home to his parents."

"Wait up!" I yelled.

Ever since the end of gym, Cheryl acted as if I had done something wrong, but I didn't know what.

"Why are you mad at me?" I asked.

"Just take the damn shower next time. I'm tired of all these secrets."

"What are you guys fussin' about?" Jackie asked.

"Something in gym class," I answered.

"I don't care if you tell that I kissed the neighbor boy," Cheryl said.

Jackie and Sarah were astonished. "You kissed that ugly neighbor boy?"

"Never mind. Maggie, we have to take showers after gym," Cheryl said.

"We'll talk later?" I asked. "The buses are about to leave."

I sat in my assigned seat near the back of the bus, next to the window. Cheryl's bus pulled out behind ours. We saw each other through the windows, but she didn't smile back.

Cheryl's mama and mine were friends. I prayed that Mama wasn't home yet to answer the phone. The bus slowed to a stop in front of our house. I stretched to see if Mama's car was in the driveway but couldn't see clearly enough.

When I reached the bottom step, I saw it: that big, brown, ugly station wagon with plastic on one of the back windows.

I walked into the house, laughing with my brothers, and acted like nothing had happened.

"Maggie?" Mama called.

I froze.

"Move out of the way." Edward pushed me. "Mama, here's Maggie. Are you looking for her?"

"Yes. Tell her to come to the bedroom."

I ran to the boy's bedroom, where Edward had gone. "I'll pay you back. Just wait and see."

Mama had a look that said, *I love you, but right now you're in trouble.*

"Sit down here, next to me." She patted the mattress.

I slid onto the edge of the bed nervously while Mama opened an envelope. "Do you know what this note will tell me?"

"Huh?"

"This note came in the mail." Mama began to read it to herself. She raised her eyebrows and straightened out a fold. "'My name is Mrs. Pollock, your daughter's gym teacher. Maggie has chosen not to participate in class or to shower. She has a D in this class and is close to getting an F.'" Mama looked at me. She folded the letter, put it back in the envelope, and laid it on the dresser. "What's so hard about gym that you are flunking?"

"The uniform doesn't fit. The snaps won't stay snapped."

"Have you asked for a larger uniform?"

"No." I slumped, hoping Mama would feel sorry for me.

"It might be too late to get a larger uniform. Tomorrow, I'll take you and your brothers to school. The principal has set up a meeting with Mrs. Pollock, me, and you."

I didn't dare ask if Cheryl's mama had called. That might get me in more trouble.

Mama stood and began to walk out of the bedroom. She turned, shaking her head. "How does someone flunk gym?"

I walked out of the bedroom and bumped into Edward. Like me, he was on his way to hang up his jacket on the front porch. He must have heard every word Mama and I spoke.

Edward sniffed. "Oh, that's you." He chuckled, tossed his baseball up in the air, and caught it with his mitt.

During the summer, I'd sit in the oversized chair to write in my journal. During the fall and winter, I'd usually sit in the linen closet that was next to the bathroom, in one of the corners. With five siblings, there wasn't much room for privacy.

This time, though, I walked outside to the back porch and stood on the top step. To the right was Aunt Louise and Uncle Ted's house. There was a wooden swing in their front yard that Uncle Ted had made.

Sometimes, sitting opposite each other, us kids would swing higher than normal for this type of swing. Aunt Louise would hobble down the back porch stairs, yelling at us to stop. Anyway, that's where I'd go.

Twenty cars and trucks must have passed by. Some people waved. There wasn't much to look at, other than traffic and the tall trees across the road. The trees are so crowded that I can't see through them.

Mama stood on the top step of our house. She looked toward Uncle John and Aunt Pearl's house.

"Over here, Mama," I yelled.

"It's time to come home. Supper's ready."

"Oh God, please don't let it be beans again," I whispered, kicking rocks.

We sat around the dining room table, "Thomas scraped his plate, eating the last of the potatoes."

"You kids can clean up the table," Mama said. "And don't forget to put away the food on the stove. Maggie, you and Mary can wash the dishes."

Mama's chair rubbed against the wooden floor. "I'm going to lay down to take a nap. Don't let me sleep all night."

It was 5:00. The table was cleaned up and the food put away. After I washed the dishes, Thomas went to his bedroom to do whatever he does in there by himself. Joe and Mary laid on the floor.

"Maggie," Joe said, "the picture has too much static. Can you fix it?"

I fiddled around with the bunny ear antenna until the picture was as clear as it could get. Carefully, I stretched out on the sofa, which had three good legs and a brick that held up the back corner.

Mike and Edward came into the house, arguing over who made the last two points, and bounced their basketball. The ball bounced two times before Mike caught it, holding it between his arm and side.

I got off the sofa and hurried into the dining room. "Be quiet," I told them. "Mama's sleeping."

"Are you on punishment or gonna get a whippin'?"

The voice came from behind the sofa. When I looked up, there was Edward.

"Ha. Ha." I smirked back.

The phone rang. Then I heard bed springs in the boys' bedroom. I pushed myself up from the couch and saw Mike fling the bedroom curtain in the air. Edward pushed him aside.

"Who are you expecting a call from?" Edward asked.

He didn't answer.

We kept the phone on the receiver, not letting anyone pick it up until we made sure it was for our family.

"Shh," I whispered. "We don't want to wake Mama. This is a party line."

There were three different ring tones for our phone. Three

short rings meant the call was for Aunt Louise. One short ring was for Aunt Pearl. Two long rings were for our family. We had to listen for the pause in between.

When our phone was installed, Mama taught all of us, except the twins, how to answer it.

"Wait, Edward," I said. "It might not be for us."

The phone rang once. After two rings, it stopped. Edward and Mike went to their bedroom. They seemed disappointed.

Mike was in ninth grade. Mama allowed him to have a close female friend. Mike called her a girlfriend. Mama set a strict policy for us to date people within the same faith, COGIC. Mike and his girlfriend sat together at the varsity basketball, football, and baseball games, and at track meets. Edward, in eighth grade, liked a girl at school in his class, but Mama didn't know. Mike and Edward were trying to figure out how to use the telephone to call their girlfriends before Mama woke up.

I was in the middle of watching a TV show, hoping to stay awake for *Alfred Hitchcock Presents* Edward peeked around the corner of the dining room. He pointed toward the front bedroom.

Mama cleared her throat. I went into the bedroom like I was looking for something. "Mama, you said that you didn't want to sleep all night."

She turned the clock to see the time. "What is everyone doin'?" She asked.

"Not much. I'm watching TV and the boys are in the back."

"Hand me my Bible," Mama said. "It's sitting on the corner of the dresser. I'll bet the boys are hoping I'm still asleep so that they can get on the phone with their friends." Mama winked.

I smiled. "Yeah."

Leaving their bedroom, like me, my brothers were whispering. "Mama is reading her Bible and will be out soon," I told them.

Edward picked up the phone quietly, and listened in on the party line conversation. Whoever was on the other end must hung up because he dialed the first number in slow motion, holding his finished dialing and held the headset against his ear.

"You know that 8:00 is the curfew for weekends," I said, angrily.

He paid my warning no mind and put his finger up to his lips.

"Mary and Joe," I said, "get on the couch with me. Please don't tell Mama that he was on the phone."

The twins laid on the floor and looked at each other.

"I'll give you some candy tomorrow," Edward said.

Mary and Joe got up and sat next to me on the couch. I frowned at Edward. He stretched the phone cord so we couldn't hear his conversation. Muffled talking came from his bedroom.

"Sit right here," I told the twins.

When I walked into the bedroom, Mama's eyes were closed. Her Bible rested on her stomach. I took a step closer, and floor creaked. Mama began to move.

"What time is it?" Mama rubbed her eyes. "I must have closed my eyes."

"Um, just after 8:00. You can lay back down for a minute. We already cleaned the kitchen."

Mama took a nap most days after work. Every night, I prayed that Daddy would come back to help us and that Mama wouldn't be so tired. That day had not come yet.

"I'm just tired from helping clean Ms. Allison's house this week after working at the facility."

"Mama?"

"Wait a minute, Maggie. I need to talk." She sat up, her back against the headboard. "Did I hear someone on the phone?"

"No," I lied.

She pointed at the chair in front of our bedroom window. "Sit right there."

It was an old, raggedy chair. When we sat on it, the cotton pushed out, and we'd push it back in. From where I sat, I noticed the twins were still on the couch.

"I needed to read my Bible to give me religious prayer on your not dressing or showering in class," Mama said.

Nervously, I sat in the chair and prayed.

Mama lowered her head and twiddled her fingers. "I've decided you won't get a whippin', but there will be a punishment because you should have let me know sooner about the gym class problem. And showering is part of your grade. As you know, if you have a weekend punishment, that starts on Friday night after school."

"Yes, ma'am."

"No sporting events. Your phone privileges are suspended this weekend, and you can't go outside unless you have chores."

Mama began to get up from the bed. She stopped and said, "You'll have a few more weekend chores. Once we meet with Mrs. Pollock and the principal on Monday, some of these punishments might be reconsidered."

I rose up from my chair.

"Also," Mama said, "lying, and including your friends in that lying, will not be tolerated. When you see Cheryl at school, you owe her an apology."

"Yes, ma'am."

Mama ran a disciplined house and a D or F grade was not acceptable. When Mama reached our bedroom, Edward was on the phone, I was nervous for him. The only thing that separated our bedroom from the living room was a curtain where there should have been a door to shut. She turned toward it. I hurried behind her. To my surprise, Edward was sitting at the dining room table, pretending to browse through a magazine.

Mama walked past him to the kitchen to make sure we had cleaned up and put away the food. I looked back at Edward and whispered, "Remember, you owe me and the twins some candy. And when did you start reading magazines?"

Dear Diary,

Life has many challenges, and gym class is one of my biggest. But I know I will figure something out to get through this class.

Chapter 29

Gym

Today no one had to watch for the bus and the appointment with the principal wasn't canceled. Mama drove to the elementary school to drop off Thomas and the twins. "Thomas, Joe, and Mary, the principal has given permission for you to sit here until the school bell rings for class."

"Thomas, please make sure your brother and sister get to class. Afterwards, you can get to yours."

Mama drove down the S-curve hill from the elementary school to the high school. I sat in the front seat, praying for something to happen to slow down our car, like a flat tire. It didn't happen. She parked two spots away from the principal's car.

Mama believed in being punctual and arrived early for our appointment. I wasn't in a hurry. No one wanted to meet with the principal, especially with your parents.

As Mama and I walked closer to the school's front entrance, sweat dripped down my face. I looked into the principal' window to see if he and Mrs. Pollock were already meeting, but I couldn't see anything. Mama walked Mike and Edward to the school's library. "You boys can wait here until the bell rings for classes."

Mama and I walked to the principal's office."Good morning," Mama said to the secretary. "My daughter and I have a meeting with Principal Jackson and Mrs. Pollock."

"Your name?" Mrs. Haynes, asked.

"Oh, I'm sorry," Mama said. "My name is Mrs. Hammond, and this is my daughter, Maggie Hammond."

"Yes," Mrs. Haynes said. "I see your name here. Principal Jackson is in the office, but we're waiting for Mrs. Pollock. Please have a seat."

From his office, the principal had a full view of the buses and guests. When the bell rang for classes, he'd stand close to the windows with his arms folded to see if anyone was running late.

I was happy our appointment was a half hour before school started and prayed it would be done before the bell rang. I didn't want anyone to see me and Mama sitting in one of the three chairs.

We sat with our backs to the office window. People said, "Good morning, Mrs. Pollock." She came into the office and sat in a chair facing us.

"Good morning," Mama said. She patted my leg. "Good morning," I whispered.

Mrs. Pollock and Mama looked up at the clock. Mrs. Haynes looked over the top of her glasses at the three of us and smiled.

After a few minutes, the principal walked toward us. "Good morning, Mrs. Hammond, Mrs. Pollock, and Maggie. I'll be with you in a minute," the principal said. He then turned toward Mrs, Haynes. "Do I have any messages?"

"One from Johnny Atkins' parents."

"I can call them later," the principal said. "Well, I see that I have a meeting scheduled for the three of us. I'll be right with you."

The principal walked into his office and sat down behind his desk. He picked up some papers and read them.

"Mrs. Pollock, Principal Jackson would like to see you first," Mrs. Haynes said.

Mrs. Pollock stood up and straightened her skirt.

Judging from Mrs. Pollock's hand gestures, it seemed as though the meeting wasn't going her way. The principal leaned into his desk, sometimes clasping his hands.

"Their meeting is taking a long time," I whispered to Mama, "The buses will be comin' in a few minutes."

"Shhh," Mama said.

The hands on the clock weren't moving fast enough. The principal swiveled his chair. He waved for Mama and me to come into his office. Mrs. Pollock stayed.

"Maggie, I understand you're not participating in gym because of the uniforms. Is that correct?"

A man was the last person I wanted to talk to about gym attire. I slumped in my chair.

"Principal Jackson," Mama said, "I don't think this meeting was thought out properly." She glanced at Mrs. Pollock. "This is a delicate subject. Maybe we should have met with Mrs. Pollock alone."

Mrs. Pollock smirked. "I haven't had any complaints."

"Could it be that the other girls are afraid to speak up?" Mama asked.

"Mrs. Hammond," the principal said. "Mrs. Pollock."

The first school bell rang. I turned around. Mike and Edward were leaving the library. They headed down the hall to their lockers and caught up with their friends. The buses continued to pull up to the school and kids gathered together.

"I understand," the principal said. "Mrs. Pollock, please work with Mrs. Hammond and Maggie. Let me know the outcome," Principal Jackson said.

Classes would start at 9:00 with the second bell. I squirmed in my seat, hoping the meeting would be over before then.

The brakes on bus 8 squeaked as it parked. Jackie, Sarah, and Cheryl walked to the front door, talking and laughing.

They stood a few feet away from the principal's office window when I heard Sarah yell, "Stop!" She pointed. "Mrs. Pollock, Maggie, and her mama are in the office."

I tried to sink further into my chair.

The principal dismissed Mama, me, and Mrs. Pollock. We couldn't hear what my friends were saying. The conversation took a few minutes when Mrs. Pollock walked back to us.

"Let's walk down the hallway toward the gym," Mrs. Pollock said. "It's too late to get a larger gym suit. What if Maggie wears a school t-shirt?"

Mama thought but didn't say anything. "Wouldn't Maggie stand out even more . . . the only one wearing a t-shirt?"

"You're right, Mrs. Hammond," Mrs. Pollock said. "What other solution could there be?"

"How about I take the gym suit home? I can fix it."

I was distracted by Cheryl, Sarah, and Jackie. They stood by the library and waited. "Go away," I mouthed at them.

"Maybe we should go to my office," Mrs. Pollock said. She looked at my friends. "There are less distractions."

As we got closer to Mrs. Pollock's office, Mama held onto my shoulder. "Will that work? You'll participate in class?"

"That . . . that'll work."

"Maggie, you will have to shower," Mrs. Pollock said as she sat at her desk. "Wearing a gym suit is part of the grade."

"Yes. I'll shower."

"Excellent," Mrs. Pollock said. "I'll let the principal know that we have solved this problem."

"Now, go and get your gym suit," Mama said. "I'll fix it tonight. Hurry up so you won't be late to class."

Mama and I walked past Mrs. Pollock's office. Mrs. Pollock stopped us. "Maggie, today you won't have to participate in class, and it will not reflect in your grade. You can participate by taking attendance, handing out towels, checking who took a shower, and things like that. Tomorrow you'll be expected to participate with the rest of the class. Is that acceptable?"

"Yes," I said.

"Maggie," Mama said. "Get to class."

I watched one more second Mama talking to the secretary to make an appointment. She'd been to the school for us kids many times. Not to say how right we were, but solved our problems.

The hallway was full of kids. I met up with Jackie and Sarah at Cheryl's locker. Cheryl and I looked at each other in silence.

"Cheryl, I'm sorry for your punishment," I said. "I shouldn't have included you in my problem."

Cheryl didn't say anything.

I thought my apology would be accepted, since Cheryl and I had waved at each other after church last Sunday and made eye contact when Mama and I sat in the principal' office.

Jackie nudged Cheryl's elbow.

"I'm *really* sorry," I said.

Cheryl held her books across her chest. She sighed. "I guess I'll accept your damn apology. But don't you ever make me help you again like that."

"I promise."

"Okay. Enough of that. What happened in the principal'
office?" They asked.

"Shoot, the second bell just rang," I said. "I'll see y'all at
lunch."

The hall emptied. Cheryl, Jackie, and I went to history
class. Sarah went to her English class.

After history class, Cheryl and I had gym. Our lockers were
next to each other and in front of Mrs. Pollock's office window.
There wasn't enough time for me to whisper and tell the whole
story to Cheryl.

Mrs. Pollock tapped on her office window. She handed a
clipboard to me to take attendance and reminded me of the other
responsibilities.

I held the locker room door open. "All right, everyone," I
hollered. "Time for gym." I checked the locker room to make sure
everyone had left. Only a few questioned why I didn't dress for
gym.

"Today, Maggie is excused from gym participation," Mrs.
Pollock said. "She will help me. Are there any questions?"

There was silence. A few boys peeked around the curtain

that separated the boys' and girls' gym classes.

"Boys do you want to join the girls' gym class? Please stop peeking around the curtain. Girls, beginning tomorrow, your lockers will be reassigned. Please see me after class for your new locker number."

We looked around at each other. I shrugged my shoulders. I hoped Cheryl recognized that I was just as surprised as she was by the announcement. Chatter echoed throughout our side of the gym. The boys peeked around the curtain again, wondering what was going on, until we heard Mr. Loren's voice. "Unless you boys want to join the girls' class, please get away from the curtain and pay attention. Mrs. Pollock already gave you the exact same warning."

After the exercise portion of the class, the girls played basketball. Cheryl moved close to me during the game, but I couldn't say anything. Mrs. Pollock kept an eye on me.

When class ended, Mrs. Pollock blew her whistle. "Hustle to the locker room!" she yelled. "It's time to hand out your locker numbers."

I was the last one into the locker room and stood next to Mrs. Pollock, but not close enough to see the locker numbers.

"Chrissy, your locker number is four. Janice, number

eight." Mrs. Pollock paused. "Maggie, your locker number is fifty."

I was happy because now I wouldn't have to walk between all the girls with a towel wrapped around me, hiding my body.

"Cheryl, you're number fifty-one."

Mrs. Pollock smiled and continued.

"Is this because of the meeting?" Cheryl whispered to me.

"We didn't talk about lockers. All I know is I don't have to walk past the girls coming out of the shower."

Susan's mouth dropped open so wide you could put a golf ball inside. "But Mrs. Pollock, that's my locker!" she said.

"Stop making such a fuss and close your mouth," Mrs. Pollock said "You can follow me to your locker."
Susan groaned.

"This should help your grades," Cheryl said to me.

"We shouldn't have to lie about being late to class," I said.

"Susan," Mrs. Pollock said, "this will be your new locker."

"Mrs. Pollock!" Susan said. "Why do I get her locker?" She pointed at me.

"This is not your decision," Mrs. Pollock said.

All the girls in the locker room listened to Mrs. Pollock and Susan argue. Susan looked at Mrs. Pollock and said, "We'll see how my father feels about this."

"All of the girls are changing lockers, not just you," Mrs. Pollock said.

After school, I skipped into the house and plopped my books on the table. Mama was in the kitchen, finishing supper.

We began to talk about school. Mama wanted to know how everything went after the meeting with Mrs. Pollock and with gym.

"Mrs. Pollock, assigned everyone in gym class new lockers."

"Oh," Mama said.

"We all have new lockers. Mine is right in front of the shower near the back of the room."

"Are you happy? I wasn't aware of the not showering."

"Well, Mrs. Pollock gave me Susan Miller's locker. Susan wasn't happy."

"I fixed your gym suit," Mama said. "Go and try it on."

I ran into the bedroom to change as fast as I could and then ran out of the bedroom. "Mama!" I was so excited. "It fits perfect."

We hugged so tightly. "Remember to take it to school with you tomorrow. You're growing so," Mama said.

"I'll help with dinner."

The next morning at school, I had the biggest smile on my face when I walked over to Cheryl. I told her about my gym suit and apologized again. We laughed on the way to our new lockers. Then we noticed other girls watching our every step. They whispered into each other's ears.

Cheryl and I began to wonder. We walked closer to our new lockers.

"Oh my God!" Cheryl said. "Do you see what I see?"

Susan was still at her old locker, undressed, as if she didn't care.

"Didn't Mrs. Pollock assign you a different locker yesterday?" I asked.

She didn't answer or make eye contact.

"Did you hear me?"

Susan slammed the locker door.

"Mrs. Pollock," I said. "Susan didn't change lockers. She went into the gym."

Mrs. Pollock hurried into the gym. "Susan, in my office. Now."

I walked fast right behind them. I sat on the bench by my old locker, wanting to hear everything. Their words were muffled, but I witnessed was Mrs. Pollock pointing her finger toward the lockers.

"Follow me, Maggie, and don't forget your new lock," Mrs. Pollock said.

Susan stomped behind Mrs. Pollock with her arms folded. Mrs. Pollock and I stood in front of my new locker, waiting for Susan to take her personal belongings out. She took her time. Every time she reached for an article of clothing, she glared back at me.

"How long does it take to grab a slip, skirt, and blouse?" I said.

"I just want to make sure this is everything," she said. She walked away with a cold stare and brushed against my shoulder.

By the time we got to the gym, our class was exercising. We hurried to stand in our spots. I glanced at Cheryl, giving her an "it's okay" look.

Teams were assigned for dodgeball. When Cheryl and I were out of the game, we got to talk.

"What happened in the locker room with Susan?" Cheryl asked. "That was crazy."

I glanced at Susan. "She just didn't want to change lockers with me, but Mrs. Pollock made her."

"Don't pay Susan no mind. She's never cared much for colored folks. None of her family does. I'm glad she's on your team."

"Why?"

"Because otherwise she'd probably try to throw that damn ball at your head and say she didn't mean to."

It took a week before I felt comfortable taking a shower. Mrs. Pollock stuck her head around the corner of my locker.

"When you finish dressing, could you come to my office?"

"Cheryl, I can't be in trouble already," I said.

When I to Mrs. Pollock's office, she said, "Tell your mother that she did a good job fixing your gym suit. Your participation in gym and showering is working out. Is everything okay with the locker change?"

I remembered seeing Susan wipe down my old locker before she put her clothes inside. I thought Susan was ignorant because a lot of people had shared that locker, colored and white, from junior high through the twelfth grade. I tried not to let her antics bother me.

"Everything is okay."

When our bus stopped in front of our house, I couldn't wait

to tell Mama about gym class. Mike and Edward rushed off the bus.

"We'll beat you to Mama, Maggie," Mike said.

While they ran to the back of the house, probably figuring Mama was in the kitchen, I ran through the front door, guessing she was in the living room with the twins.

"No you won't," I replied.

The three of us entered the house at the same time. We tossed our books down and left the doors open.

"Mama!" we yelled.

If you enter our house from the back or front, you can see all the rooms except for the bedrooms and bathroom.

Mama wasn't in the bedroom. The boys didn't see her in the kitchen or dining room either. The only room left was the bathroom.

"Mama!" we yelled again. "Are you in there?"

No answer.

"Where could she be?"

The twins walked in the back door. Mama followed. All of us began to talk at once.

"Wait a minute," Mama said. "Can I get inside the house?"

"Mama, what I have to say is more important," I said.

We fought back and forth. After Mama walked into the kitchen, she reached into the bottom cabinet and grabbed a pot and top. She clapped them together until the house became quiet. The twins thought it was funny.

"Now, everyone sit at the table," Mama said. "I will listen to all of you. Maggie, you can go first."

Mike and Edward grumbled but had to listen to me anyway.

"Mama, gym class went great today. The gym suit fit perfectly, fit and I participated. My grade will go up."

"You didn't take a shower? I smell something," Edward said.

Mama didn't say a word, just gave Edward a long stare. "Go on, Maggie."

"And I showered," I looked at Edward.

"Okay boys, what do you have to say?" Mama asked.

"I made the football team," Mike said. "I'll start practice next week."

"How will you get back and forth from practice?" Mama asked. "I work at the facility when I can. And occasionally we work the fields after school."

"I'll find a way," Mike said. "Maybe I can catch Uncle Ted

before he leaves work. I haven't figured out the working in the fields part."

"Will you need money for equipment or shoes?"

"Everything will be worked out."

"Well, congratulations, Mike," Mama said. "Now you, Edward."

"I don't really have any news," Edward said. "I just wanted to hear what you'd say about Mike playing football. Can I stay after school and watch?"

"What about your homework? And yours, Mike?"

"I'll make sure it's done immediately when I get home," Mike said.

"Me, too," Edward said.

"Edward, you can stay and watch, but you guys better complete your homework." Mama said.

We ran to Mama and hugged as a family.

"You kids are growing up and don't need to miss out on everything. We'll make it. Now does anyone else have any news?"

We looked around the table at each other. No one had anything else to say.

"I met the principal about the bus seating arrangements,"

Mama said. "There aren't any assigned seats for the buses. Kids that are picked up first should sit in the front seats, and so forth. Since you are picked up near the end of the route, your seats are near or in the back."

"But Mama, every year?" Mike said.

"This might not seem fair, but are there many kids."

"A couple," Edward said.

"For now, that is the answer. Let me know if there are any other changes to the bus where you feel discriminated."

"Okay," Mike said.

"Now, help me with dinner. We're having left overs."

Mike said, "Okay."

Mama kept looking at us and heated up the food. "Maggie, go and put on one of the Mahalia Jackson songs. A happy one."

I loved Mahalia Jackson. Her albums were in most colored homes, religious or not. I let the Victrola choose the song, laying the needle somewhere on the record.

While setting the dinner table, we sung along with the record. Mama tapped her hands against the counter. Eventually, the rest of us sang or clapped their hands up until we sat at the dinner table. The house was peaceful again.

Dear Diary,

All I can think to say is thank you. Thank you for my family.

Chapter 30

Oh! Oh!

History was my favorite class, but at this moment, Mr. Michaels' voice was a muffle. I daydreamed, staring out the window, thinking of the courage I would need to finally leave a note to a boy that I like.

I thought about his family who lived in the two-story brown house on the other side of town. He was popular. I can't remember him ever teasing me because we were poor.

Someone tapped me on the shoulder. My arm that I leaned against my chin fell on my desk. And my papers scattered to the floor. When I turned, there was Bobby. "Pass this note to Tammy," he whispered.

Tammy was the girl he liked. She sat in front of me. I leaned over to pick up my papers. Kids snickered.

"Miss Hammond," Mr. Michaels said, "is there something that the class should know, or am I just boring?"

"No, Mr. Michaels. There's nothing you should know, and

you are most certainly *not* boring," I said.

The entire classroom laughed. Then the bell rang for the end of class. Kids darted from their desks like it was the end of school, but it was only lunchtime.

"Remember the homework assignment written on the chalkboard," Mr. Michaels yelled over the noise.

I tried to blend in with the crowd. I had one foot out of the classroom when I heard Mr. Michaels' voice.

"Miss Hammond!" he called.

"Shoot," I whispered, turning around. He waved his hand to come see him.

"I'll catch up with you, Cheryl. If I'm late, save me a seat."

"Maggie," Mr. Michaels said, "I've noticed you're not as focused as you used to be at the beginning of school. Is everything okay?"

"What do you mean? I'm getting a C."

"You started the class with A's and were one of my top students."

"Yes, Mr. Michaels," I said in a flat tone.

He tapped his fingers on the desk and leaned back in his chair. "You're sure everything is okay?"

Although I reassured him, he tapped his fingers on the desk and leaned back in his chair.

"You're sure everything is okay?" he repeated.

"Yes."

"Well, I guess there's not much else for me to say."

"Am I excused?"

"Wait one moment. Next time you daydream, could you please let the entire class know what's more intriguing outside than in my classroom?"

I grimaced, unsure of what to say.

Once Mr. Michaels excused me, I hurried in between the kids in the hallway.

Cheryl waited for me at her locker. "Come on," she yelled, "before we lose our spot at the lunch table."

I opened my locker and grabbed the note I had written. An aroma past by me. Lifting my head, I closed my eyes and sniffed into the air.

That smell could only belong to one person: Raymond Grant. It meant his father, who traveled from time to time, must be home. He'd bring back gifts, one being men's cologne that wasn't sold in local stores, and Raymond wore some of them to school.

"Sorry, Maggie," Raymond said. "I didn't mean to bump into you."

I smiled and tried not to act like a lovesick girl. "Oh, that's all right."

My eyes followed him and his friends all the way to his locker.

"Could you be any more obvious?" Cheryl nudged me. "Hurry up."

"If you'd stop lookin' at the fella while tryin' to open your locker, you'd get to lunch much faster," Edward said.

"Cheryl, touch my forehead," I said. "Maybe I'm hearing things. Was that Edward, my brother, who told me the rules of walking in the same hallway with him, for me to never tell anyone that I was his little sister?"

"Your brother seems friendly and all," Cheryl said, "but I don't understand him. He's weird."

Sarah and Jackie yelled and waved their arms in the air. "Cheryl and Maggie!"

I tossed the note on the top shelf of my locker. When I closed my locker, I nicked the top of my finger. I fought the urge to holler, wondering if Raymond had seen me.

Cheryl chuckled. "Don't worry, your knight in shining armor looked but didn't laugh. He's walking toward the cafeteria."

I had kept the note a secret from Sarah and Jackie. They both had big mouths and would tell Raymond.

"Who are you peeping at?" Sarah asked.

I didn't answer her. I checked the hallway, wanting to make sure it was clear of students before I tried to put the note inside his locker. There were three small openings on the front of our lockers, so I would have to be fast and pray the note wouldn't slip out.

"What are you waiting for?" Cheryl asked. "This is the best time. Everyone has gone to line up for lunch."

As I got closer to his locker, my heart began to beat faster. My hands were sweating.

"Hurry up," Cheryl said.

I took a deep breath and told myself to do it. I slipped the note between the slits of the locker and heard someone leave the math room.

Trying not to panic, I walked toward my friends as they called out my name. I got around the corner, stopped near the end of the lunch line, and leaned against the wall, nervous.

"What's wrong with you?" Sarah asked.

"Did. . ." I caught my breath. "Did anyone see me slide the note inside Raymond's locker?"

"No," Cheryl said.

"Are you sure?"

Cheryl nodded. "You're one of the shyest and quietest girls in class. How did you get the courage to do such a thing?"

"What?" Sarah asked.

Pointing a finger at Sarah and Jackie, I said, "Do *not* tell him my secret, or I'll tell yours." They turned around and walked closer to the lunch room with me and Cheryl.

The lunchroom was surrounded by floor-to-floor ceiling windows on one side and the gymnasium, also referred to as the auditorium, on the other.

At noon, smells from the lunch room filled the hallways. The fifty kids from the junior high school enjoyed forty-five minutes of not having to think about math, science, history or English.

Cheryl and Jackie walked to our usual table. I lingered by the school's athletic trophy case, standing on my tiptoes to see if Raymond and his friends sat at their usual table in the corner.

"Come on, Maggie!" Jackie hollered. "Someone has

already taken one of our seats."

I looked to see what Jackie was talking about. A group of girls had sat in all but three of our seats. That meant that if we gossiped about anything. Sarah was going to have to lean across the table to hear over the noise.

The girl next to us was Shannon. I stood behind her and cleared my throat. "Um-hum. Excuse me. Would you mind trading seats across the table so that our friend can sit next to us? She's in line getting her lunch."

She acted like she didn't hear me.

I tapped her shoulder. "Excu-"

"I heard you the first time," she said. She tilted her head from one side to the other. "Um ... no. I don't think so." She turned back around and laughed with her friends.

"Sarah is just gonna just have to sit across from us today," I said. I looked in my lunch bag to see what Mike had fixed for today's lunch. "Thank God. Peanut butter and jelly. No potted meat."

"So?" Cheryl asked.

"So what?" I asked back.

"You never told us what you wrote in the note," Cheryl

said.

I took a bite of my sandwich. "Um-hum."

"Well, did you at least sign it?"

I still didn't answer.

"Maggie," Cheryl whispered, "look at me. I'm your best friend."

"Shh," I said. Didn't she realize the people around us would overhear?

Sarah walked up to the table. *Thank God. What good timing.*

"What did I miss?" Sarah asked. "And where's my seat?"

We pointed toward her seat. She walked around the table with a frown, eyes focused on Shannon, mumbling to herself. Then she sat down across from me. "Maggie," she said. "I still can't believe you gave him a note."

Shannon looked at us, wondering what we were talking about.

I decided to walk to the bathroom. I asked Sarah to come with me. "Sarah," I said, "please be quiet. This is why I didn't want you to know anything."

"And why not me? Because you've always been shy when

it comes to boys . . . you know . . . being so sanctified and filled with the Holy Ghost and all."

For some reason, my friends thought that because I attend church, I can't like boys.

"My mama lets my older brothers date girls," I said.

"That's different, they're boys. You know good and well that she isn't gonna let you date or have a boyfriend. He might not even read the note."

I decided that before lunch was over, I'd return to my locker a little earlier. The note was written on pink paper. When Raymond opened his locker, the note should fall onto his face. Cheryl bugged me about if the note was signed.

After sneaking a look at Raymond, I whispered, "No. The note was signed 'your secret admirer, M'. Now stop bugging me."

"M?" Sarah whispered loudly. "How will he know what 'M' means?"

We waited for Jackie to finish her lunch. Then someone shoved me while I was standing. My half-full glass of Kool-Aid spilled onto my skirt. When I turned around there was Sarah.

"Why did you do that?" I asked.

"Stop staring at the boy. You're acting like someone who

has never had a crush."

Sarah's family wasn't as conservative as mine. They went to other people's house parties, to the bars in Idlewild, and invited people over to their house for drinks. Sarah had a boyfriend, Anthony, but I'm not sure if her family knew about them kissing. Sarah acted like it didn't matter. To be honest, I was jealous. Now, she didn't know that we all knew that she and Anthony had a big fight, so this was the perfect time.

"So, Sarah, tell us, how are you and Anthony doing?" I asked. "Didn't you two lovebirds have a big fight? Did you make up yet?"

Sarah didn't know that we knew. She squeezed to get out of the line.

While we were fighting, Raymond and his friends headed outside with a football. I heard Raymond yell, "Stop that running play!"

I waited until he came back inside. He walked briskly, and I stayed close enough behind him to see when he reached his locker.

Cheryl and I waited for the moment the note would fall out of his locker. He took his time at his locker. I tried to open my locker but got the combination wrong. It didn't help that I kept looking back at Raymond.

His locker opened. One of his friends came up behind him and pushed him into his locker. The note fell onto the floor. My eyes opened wide, and I looked at Cheryl. She covered her mouth with her hands.

It seemed like the note would end up down the hall. Kids stepped on it and pushed it with their feet. Raymond must have noticed the bright pink paper. He picked it up. My heart pounded. My hands were sweaty. I stood still, fumbling with my lock. He read the note and folded it back up.

When he began to look around, I panicked. I turned my head, hoping he believed that the note came from someone else.

Then Misty Johnson walked up to him, smiling. He smiled back and flashed the paper at her. He didn't let her read it, but that didn't matter. They both smiled.

The bell rang and the hallway cleared. Raymond and Misty walked in different directions. Cheryl and I attended class.

"You have to do something," Cheryl said.

"Like what?"

"You know how the principal spoke to the junior high about the annual sports challenge?"

"Yeah."

"Well, you can impress him with your running, you know, when you beat all the girls. You'll be the center of attention. I'm sure Misty won't participate. She has no athletic skills whatsoever."

"You might be right." I smiled.

Dear Diary,

Raymond read the note. He didn't know it was from me. I have decided to compete in the junior high sports challenge.

Chapter 31

Sports?

The whispers are that Principal Smith has been talking about a junior high sport challenge to help the morale between the sixth, seventh, and eighth graders.

In my mind, nothing was going to help the morale. We'd always be sixth graders to the seventh graders and to the eighth graders, who felt a sense of entitlement anyway because they were one step away from saying, "I'm in high school and you're not."

Once home, I plopped my books on the bed.

"Where's Mama?" I asked. No one answered me except Mary said.

"She went outside to get the clothes off the clothesline," Mary said

Mama grabbed a handful of our bedsheets.

"Can I participate in the junior high sports challenge next week Friday?" I asked her.

Mama gave me an encouraging smile and hug. "Yes,

you can, but I'm not sure if I can make it. I'll see if one of your brothers can be there. Someone has to watch the twins."

Mama had not seen me race before except outside in front of the house on the dirt road with my brothers and, sometimes, with the neighbors.

"I hope you can make it," I said.

"Help me with the sheets. Then go and look on the bed." She smiled. "Someone sent you something."

I ran into the house, letting the door slam. Mama didn't even holler.

"What's wrong with you?" Mary asked.

I plopped onto the bed, stomach first, smiling. Janet had written me a letter. After she had left, we had promised to keep in touch with each other. The letter read:

Dear Maggie,

I really enjoyed meeting you this summer and spending time with you and writing in our diaries. White Cloud is so different than where I live down south. This was my first summer in your town, and I wasn't sure what my experience was going to be. But after I met you, Cheryl, and your sister, it was really wonderful. In my family, I'm the only girl. Tell your sister and Cheryl hello for me, and to keep writing in their diaries. Well, I have to go. Save me some cherries, okay?

Janet

"Mary!" I hollered. "Come in here."

"I'm watching TV."

"Come here!"

"What you want?"

"Janet wrote me a letter. I can't read all of it to you, but she told me to tell you hello and to keep writing in your diary."

We hollered back and forth until Mary finally came into the bedroom, wanting to read the letter. She tried to reach each word while I held my finger underneath it.

Once Mary had finished, she asked me about the race. "Are you excited?"

"Yes, I'm excited, but I'm nervous at the same time. It will be in front of all of the junior high, including Raymond."

"No one will catch you," Mary said.

Mama came inside and put the remainder of the sheets and towels away. Mike followed her and called everyone to the table for dinner.

• • • •

The next week, on Friday, the halls were buzzing about the sports challenge. Kids were saying how they were going to beat this person and the other.

The boys and girls competed on consecutive Fridays with a ribbon ceremony at the end of the competition. Today was the girls' competition. Principal Jackson spoke into the intercom. "The girls who will be participating in the junior high sports challenge are excused from class and should report to the gym."

This year, I had mastered the quick walk. That's when a student walks fast, but not too fast that a teacher yells, "Slow down!" Cheryl and the rest of my friends had practiced this in the hallway.

"The remainder of the junior high are to line up behind your class teachers and follow them to the gym," Principal Jackson said, "Sixth graders will go first. Once they are in the gym, the seventh graders can go, and then the eighth graders."

Some parents sat in the middle of the bleachers. Although Jackie wasn't racing, her mother came. Her father didn't. He worked at the local factory. Daddy worked on the railroad in Chicago, so I knew he couldn't make it.

"Okay, girls," Mrs. Pollock said. "You can go into the gym."

Each class sat on the bleachers in their designated sections. There were twenty girls who participated and waited in the locker room until it was time to race. We then came out and sat in the bottom three rows until our race was called.

I turned to look for Raymond, trying to be as unsuspecting as possible. He was sitting in the middle row, among his friends, with the sixth graders.

Mrs. Pollock stood in the middle of the gym. "There will be two events: basketball and track. Since there isn't much time, basketball will play a half-court game. The first to ten wins the game."

The sixth graders walked out onto the court with confidence, smiling. Five minutes into the game, the smiles began to disappear. The seventh and eighth graders beat us in basketball. We walked off the court with our heads down.

Our families cheered us on, saying, "You'll get them in track."

"Maggie can run faster than any of them," Edward said. He

pointed toward me, smiling.

The last event was indoor track. There were two participants from each class with only one winner.

Susan and I were the sixth grade runners, April and Cassie the seventh grade runners, and Gail and Norma the eighth grade runners. We walked to the starting line.

Cheryl, Sarah, and Jackie shouted, "You can beat them, Maggie!"

We had to run three times around the gym. I felt myself getting nervous and tired, barely beating the other girls in the semifinals. I didn't want to lose this race, especially against Susan. There was a break in between the races for us to rest before running the last laps.

I was in the start position. I looked to my left at Gail, and then I glared at Susan, who was to my right. Mrs. Pollock raised her arm. "On your mark." She paused. "Get set." Another pause, longer than the first one. "Go."

I jumped at the sound of the whistle. It took me half a lap before I caught up to Gail and Susan and took the lead. Susan and Gail passed me in the second lap. Coming to the last curve, I saw Edward in the stands. He waved his arms in a forward motion, encouraging me.

My legs hurt below the knee. I grimaced, sweat dripping down my face. I remembered how my brothers and I raced up and down the dirt road on Rural Route 1 in front of our house and in the tall grassy fields across the road. I thought, *Gail might beat me, but not Susan.*

Gail neared the curve before the long stretch to the finish line. Susan wasn't far behind Gail. I was in third place, believing I could catch up. My arms tightened as I came to the last curve.

Families and kids cheered. I glanced up at the bleachers but didn't see my friends. When I was racing down the straightaway, I saw Jackie, Sarah, Cheryl, and Edward near the finish line.

"Run, Maggie!" they shouted.

Edward showed me again how to use my arms, moving them back and forth. I mimicked his movements, stretched my legs, and tried hard not to think about the pain. I gasped for air, crossing the finish line in second place, bent over with my hands on my knees. Susan placed third and Gail finished first.

Cheryl, Sarah, and Jackie hugged me.

"Good job, sis."

The voice wasn't very loud, but sincere. I slowly looked up

and saw Edward. He walked me to the bleachers and encouraged me to stretch my legs. I gasped again in pain, and he helped rub the cramps out of my legs.

Mrs. Pollock began to walk across the gym toward me. "Maggie, I didn't know you could run so fast. You ran a good race."

Edward kept rubbing my cramped legs and looked up at me.

"Hey, are you okay?" Mrs. Pollock asked.

When I turned around, I saw Gail, the eighth grader who had won the race.

"Yeah," I said.

"If it hadn't been for those darn cramps," I told myself.

We laughed. Gail teased me about how my brother helped rub cramps from my legs. We turned around and noticed Susan at the other end of the bleacher.

"That is one unhappy girl," I said.

Gail said, "A girl on the track team is moving out of town. I hope Mrs. Pollock will ask you to take her place."

That really surprised me.

Edward helped me to the girls' locker room and then turned to leave, but not before telling me, "make sure you want to run track with the junior high because it won't be just our school running. There's a lot of competition."

I smiled and nudged the door open to the locker room, but not before peeking through the crack of the door at Susan. She vented her frustration to whomever listened.

"I don't like to lose to anyone, especially a colored girl," she said.

When Cheryl and I entered the locker room, Susan threw her towel on the floor.

"Susan, Maggie beat you fair and square," Mrs. Pollock said.

"Maggie," Mrs. Pollock said. "Have you ever thought about joining the junior high track team?"

My mouth dropped open. I looked around at the other girls and then at Gail.

"What?" Susan said.

"I - I guess so," I stuttered. "I'll have to ask my mama."

"Let me know as soon as possible. The track team meets every Monday, Tuesday, and Wednesday. The last track meet is in one week, here at the school." She asked me to check with Mama to see if I could come watch the race. If Mama approved, I could start next season, in January. After changing my clothes, I ran out of the locker room to find Cheryl. She had already left.

I slowed down to a brisk walk. Cheryl and Jackie stood outside the front door of the school. I waved my hands, and Cheryl waved back.

"You guys won't believe what just happened," I said.

They gave me a questioning look.

"Mrs. Pollock just asked me to join the junior high track team."

I thought Cheryl would jump up and down. Instead, her smile changed to a frown. Jackie and Sarah also frowned.

"Did you guys hear what just happened?"

"So, all of this excitement isn't that Raymond found out you wrote the note?" Jackie asked.

"No. You guys aren't excited about my track news? This is Mrs. Pollock, the one who gave me nightmares about not wearing my gym uniform."

"Come on, Maggie." Sarah said.

"Maggie, don't feel bad," she said. " Sarah and Jackie aren't in our gym class. They don't know the whole story about the gym uniform. And, Mrs. Pollock is speaking to you differently, a little nicer, since she saw you run."

"Cheryl," I said. "You're being silly. As odd as it might seem, I can't wait to run and compete against someone other than my brothers and neighbors and win."

There were whispers about June, an eighth grader and the only colored girl on the team. I had seen her run and heard she's fast and helped the track team win a lot of meets. Not sure where she was today because she wasn't at the meet.

Sarah said, "You're gonna be the next token. That one n-" She paused. "The colored girl to help them win. You know I'm right."

"Mama always tells us not to look at life as if we're the next token," I said. "She tells us to learn everything we can so that when we grow up and have families, we won't have to pick crops every summer."

"Are you girls riding the bus or not?" Our bus drivers yelled.

"I can't miss the bus," I said. "Talk to you guys later."

Cheryl and Jackie ran to their buses. Sarah sat on the bench in front of the school, waiting for her mother to pick her up.

On the bus, I sat in my assigned seat near the back, next

to the window. I couldn't wait to get home and tell Mama about the race today and that Mrs. Pollock wanted me to be on the track team. Through the window, I saw Cindy, an upper classman who was assigned the seat next to me on the bus. She wasn't walking with any sense of urgency. The bus driver began to close the door in slow motion to see if anyone else would run out of the school.

Cindy didn't move toward the bus, so I got to sit near the aisle and not by the window.

The seven miles home seemed longer than usual. I counted every stop and watched the door open and close until the school bus came to a stop in front of the family's brown shingled house on Rural Route 1. There were four stops remaining and less than a mile to go.

I leaned into the aisle, on the edge of my seat. Mr. Hucklebee kept an eye on me.

"Miss Hammond," he shouted, "please sit back in your seat. If I brake, you'll fly to the front of the bus."

I scooted back in my seat until the doors of the bus opened. I rushed down the steps, only to slip on our gravel driveway. I hurried into the house, wanting to be the first to catch Mama's attention and tell her my news.

My brothers ran past me to the back door. I didn't follow them, choosing instead to run through the front porch. I saw Mama in the kitchen cooking. I threw my books on the chair in the living room and hollered her, "Mama!"

"Kids, why are you runnin' through the house, hollerin' like there's a fire?"

I tried to get all of my words out first. "Mama, I ran the race today and came in second place!" Breathing even harder, I said, "And Mrs. Pollock asked me to join the track team!"

"Calm down, child. What do you mean a track team?"

"There's a track team for the junior high girls, and Mrs. Pollock asked me to join. I wouldn't have to worry about a track uniform or anything. All I need is a white t-shirt and blue shorts."

"You mean the same Mrs. Pollock who gave us a hard time about your gym uniform and numerous other problems?"

"She has changed, Mama," I said. "Remember how I told you that she has been nicer to me and changed the lockers?"

"Oh, Maggie," Mama said. "My work hours are hectic, and I'm not sure how you'd get home from practice, the meets and-"

"The meets are after school, and we only have one a week. Maybe Uncle Ted could give me a ride home. I could do my homework while waitin' for him to get out of work."

Mama wanted to know what other schools I'd run against. She looked concerned. "What if the other team trips you or calls you a nigger?"

"We'll run against Baldwin, Grant, Newaygo, and Fremont . . ." I paused to think. "There might be another one. Oh yeah, Hesperia."

Mama stopped mixing the cornbread batter and wiped her hands on her apron. "Let's talk to uncle Ted before any decision is made. When does practice start?"

Edward and Mike interrupted. "Mama, we have some news too, about basketball tryouts."

"What!" Mama said, "Mike, aren't you still playing football?"

"Mama, can I run track?" I asked.

"Just one minute, Mike. Let Maggie finish telling me about this track team."

My brothers gave me angry looks, moving their lips, but I couldn't make out what they were saying.

"The track team only has one meet left this year, so I wouldn't start practice until January," I said. "They need one more girl because one might drop out."

"Dinner is at Uncle Ted and Aunt Louise's house on Saturday evening. I'll, I mean we'll, ask him then."

Edward leaned against his bedroom doorway, arms crossed, and giving me the evil eye. I smelled fried chicken and collard greens and heard the sizzle of cornbread batter hitting the grease in the skillet. On the counter were two homemade pies: apple and peach.

At the dinner table, we had meetings and got to share something exciting that had happened to them during the day.

Mama went around the table. "Mary and Joe, do you have anything you'd like the family to know?"

Joe looked at Mary and shook his head. Mary stumbled over her words. "Well, I like my teacher. Is that something good?"

"Thomas, do you have anything you'd like to say?" Mama asked.

"Nah. Except school was school, and boring."

I said, "I've been asked to run on the track team. I just need to work out some arrangements with Mama and Uncle Ted."

"Well, I thank the Lord for continuing to give us have a roof over our heads and food on the table," Mama said. "If no one else has anything to say, we can clean the table."

Cleaning the table was the quickest job to do, so I sought Thomas to make a deal. "You know, Thomas," I said. "tomorrow is your day to mop the kitchen floor."

"What deal are you tryin' to make now?" Thomas asked.

"If you wash the dishes tonight, I'll mop the kitchen floor for you tomorrow."

He thought about it for five seconds. "Okay, it's a deal. What are you in a hurry to do?"

"I want to write my friend Janet a letter that has to get in the mail tomorrow." I sat on the front porch in the oversized chair, opened my school notebook, and wrote:

Dear Janet,

Today, some of the junior high kids raced against each other. Our principal created a sporting challenge in the hopes that we'd get to know each other better. Personally, I think it's a waste of time, but we got out of class. More exciting than that is I got second place in a race, beating all but one eighth grader. My gym teacher, the one who's been giving me grief, even moved my gym locker closer to the showers because of Mama's complaint with my gym suit and girls staring at my breasts.

Now, let me tell you about Raymond, the boy that I like. I didn't know how to get his attention, so I slid a note into his locker. It has been a few days, and he hasn't noticed me. I guess it would have helped if I had signed my name instead of just putting an M. I guess what Raymond did notice is how fast I ran. I'm hoping that will help, since he likes sports.

Cheryl said to say hello. She's still working on what you told us to do to conquer junior high.

Sincerely Maggie

Chapter 32

Saturday Dinner?

Saturday morning, I sat on the front porch and waited for Mr. Peterson, the mailman. It didn't take long before his truck stopped three houses up the road at Mrs. Ollies' house. I ran outside and stood in front of our mailbox with Janet's letter in hand.

Usually, if Mama had something to mail, she'd ask us to raise the red mailbox flag in an upward position. But I wanted to hand-deliver my letter to Mr. Peterson to make sure it didn't get left in the back of the mailbox.

"Good morning, Maggie." Mr. Peterson smiled.

"I have a letter to mail. It's to my friend down south. Will you make sure it gets mailed?"

"I'll do my best. Anything else going out?"

"No," I replied.

Before driving off, Mr. Peterson handed me one envelope.

. . . .

It was close to 4:00 when Granddaddy, Grandma, Uncle John, Aunt Pearl, and our family met at Uncle Ted's house for a Saturday dinner.

When we had finished eating, Uncle Ted sat in his favorite rocking chair on the front porch. While I helped clean the kitchen, I kept looking around the corner toward the porch.

Mama and I walked out to the front porch, passing between Aunt Louise and the rest of the grownups in the dining room who were talking and playing a board game.

Mama sat in the other rocking chair near Uncle Ted. I sat on the top step.

"Hey," he said. "Looks cloudy over there. Might get some rain."

Mama and I looked to where he pointed near the trees across the road. She nudged my shoulder.

"Uncle Ted?" I hesitated, nervous to speak.

"Go ahead," Mama whispered.

I fiddled with my fingers, hoping not to stumble over my words.

Uncle Ted noticed I was nervous. He peered over the top of

his glasses. "I understand you want to run track."

"Yes. I do."

"You think those skinny legs can run fast enough?"

Uncle Ted's noticed I was nervous. He peered at me over the top of his glasses. "I understand that you want to run track?" His voice reminded me of a warm summer breeze. It was calm and easygoing, and he always smiled. I smiled back. "Not only can they run fast enough, but they can win."

"And what is it you need from me?" He asked, with a toothpick between his lips.

I glanced toward Mama and back at Uncle Ted. "Well, I'd really appreciate it, and I promise to do my homework and not bug anyone at the courthouse if you could give me a ride home from practice."

"You'll have to sit in my office until I've finished cleaning the entire couthouse," Uncle Ted said.

"I promise."

"How many days do you practice?"

"Three days a week. Monday and Tuesday. Wednesday is the day we have the track meets."

"What schools will you run against . . . I mean, beat?"

Uncle Ted smiled.

"Baldwin, Grant, Newaygo, Fremont, and Hesperia. Mrs. Pollock said that since the team's bus will pass our house from Hesperia, they'd drop me off at home."

"As long as you follow the rules while I'm at work and try your hardest to win some meets, I'll give you a ride. Also, your homework has to be completed."

. . . .

It was the end of school when Mrs. Pollock told me that I would be added to the junior high track team. "Be ready for your first meet on Wednesday afternoon against Baldwin. The bus leaves right after gym class."

When Wednesday came, I ran out of the girls' locker room with one track shoe in each hand.

Mrs. Pollock and I stepped onto the bus where the other girls waited. "We thought you were gonna chicken out," someone hollered.

"Me?" I responded. "No way. I've been waiting for this day." Little did any of them know, I was actually nervous because the only girls I'd raced were from our school. Today, I'd be racing against girls I didn't know and hadn't seen, except when our church fellowshipped in Baldwin. Baldwin was about a forty-five-minute ride from White Cloud.

I stared out the window until Gail began to sing, "Baby love, oh baby love" into my ear. The rest of the track team joined in.

I shoved Gail away from me. "Why are you guys singing that song?" I asked.

"Come on," Gail said. "We all know who you like, leaving notes. You're hoping he shows up at the meet, aren't you?"

"You guys don't know what you're talkin' about. I'm just nervous." I didn't want to believe the team knew that I liked Raymond. I wasn't going to say his name and let the cat out of the bag either.

"Calm down, girls," Mrs. Pollock said. She stood in the aisle. The bus hit a bump, and she grabbed onto the seat beside her. "Like with all our other meets, we're gonna try our best to win because believe me that's what the other girls are thinking. Here are your events."

The bus drove into the Baldwin High School parking lot. The Newaygo, Grant, Hesperia, and Fremont buses were already there. Hesperia's bus parked behind ours.

"Let's stretch over here," Mrs. Pollock said.

Gail walked over to me and sat on the ground. "Don't look at none of the girls right now. Keep stretching and jog around the track with the team, but in the middle."

"Why the middle?" I asked.

"Comfort." She smiled.

Our team jogged around the track two times. The announcer said, "The high jumpers can go to the right side of the track. Anyone running the 100-yard dash can go to the start line."

Gail and I both ran the 100, along with two girls from each of the other schools.

Mrs. Pollock patted my shoulders. "You're going do just fine."

I loosened my legs, wiggled them, and stretched my arms. Gail ran with the first heat.

An announcement came over the intercom. "Runners in the next heat, please stand in your assigned lanes behind your lines."

While standing behind my line, I looked in the grandstand for my family. No one was there.

"On your mark." There was a pause. I remembered Mrs.

Pollock had told me to not focus on the pauses. "Get set." This was the shorter pause. Then a gun shot fired.

I didn't start well and slipped which put me in last place. I had to make up time.

"Run!" someone yelled. I didn't know if it was meant for me or the other girls. I pretended it was for me. I thought what Uncle Ted told me about my skinny legs and if they could win. I told him, "Yes." It was all the encouragement I needed.

When I crossed the finish line and my hands on my waist, I gasped for breath . My team rushed over. Some of the girls put their arms around me.

"You did wonderful, Maggie." Mrs. Pollock said. "I can't believe you ran so fast."

"But I didn't win, Mrs. Pollock."

"It doesn't matter. You came in third place against girls in the eighth grade from schools other than ours."

For me, third place wasn't a win. I didn't make it to the finals.

"Everyone, pay attention," Mrs. Pollock said. "One of the girls from another team has dropped out of the final race for the 100-yard dash."

"What happened, Mrs. Pollock?" Gail asked.

"I can't say right now. I was given the information by a track official. But it means that, Maggie," Mrs. Pollock turned toward me, "will run in the finals."

My eyes opened wide.

"You and Gail need to warm up. And remember that immediately afterwards, you'll have to warm up for the relay."

"Gail, how will I be ready for the relay?" I asked.

"Calm down. Right now, just think about the 100."

Gail and I jogged past the bleachers, keeping our legs warmed up. "Maybe you'll get that first place after all," Gail said.

"Good luck!" Uncle Ted sat on the top bleacher. As much as I wanted to run up to him, I couldn't risk tripping, so I kept jogging with Gail. I smiled at Uncle Ted.

Gail and I stopped jogging to watch one of our teammates high jump. I held my breath when the back of her foot touched the pole. It wobbled but didn't fall. Another teammate finished the 200-yard dash fourth place.

"Let's get back," Gail said. "They'll be announcing our race soon."

Gail and I continued to jog on the grass alongside the track when the announcer called for the 100-yard dash finalists to line up. Gail was one lane over from me. This time I was in the first lane.

I waited for the sound of the gun that signaled the beginning of the race. I moved my arms back and forth. Gail, the Baldwin girl, and I ran side by side.

Mrs. Pollock had practiced with our team on breaking away near the middle of the race. Gail ran ahead. The Baldwin girl and I were neck and neck. The crowd yelled. Gail crossed the finished line first and I was second.

I was happy because even as a sixth grader, I had beat all the eighth graders except one. I ran up the bleachers to Uncle Ted. I hoped he thought it was a good race. "Did you see how fast I ran?"

"Yes, I did." He smiled. "Next time, you'll do even better. Now make sure to let your track coach know that I'm taking you home."

I had hoped to see one other person in the grandstands. I had hoped my running would make Raymond notice me instead of passing in the hallway, bumping our shoulders against each other by mistake.

"Are you looking for anyone in particular?" Uncle Ted

asked.

"No." I climbed into his red pickup truck.

· · · ·

With Daddy gone, Uncle Ted was the male figure that I talked to the most, outside of our pastor. I wondered how to talk about boys, so I began with track.

"Uncle Ted, I want to beat all the girls on the other teams. How do you think I can do that?"

"Well, it takes a lot of practice," he said. "I've seen how you race kids up and down the road in front of the house. Why don't you race against them for practice?"

"That could work, but who will time us?"

"Do they time you in your races against the other schools?"

"Mrs. Pollock, the track coach, has a stopwatch."

Uncle Ted came up with his own stopwatch: his pocket watch. The only stop he made on the way home was at the gas station across from the airport in White Cloud. This would give me time to talk to Uncle Ted about another concern.

I cleared my throat. "Uncle Ted. I have another question."

"What's that?"

I focused on looking out the front window, so I wouldn't have to look at him. I took a deep breath, silently counted to three, and blurted out, "There's a boy at the school . . ."

Uncle Ted took his eyes off the road for a second and looked at me. "This boy goes to our church?"

"Does that matter?"

Uncle Ted glanced at me again.

"No. He doesn't go to our church."

"You're a church girl. If you were old enough to have a boyfriend, the church prefers that he attend our church or be in the same faith."

This conversation didn't seem to be going well "Does it count if he's from a nice family?"

"I think you need to focus on your books."

"Didn't you like girls when you were my age?"

"Times were different back then. And I courted the young lady. She didn't court me."

"So, I have to wait until I'm old? I'm sorry, Uncle Ted. I spoke out of turn."

Uncle Ted turned into the driveway. Before we got out of the truck, he lifted his cap and scratched his head. "All I'm sayin' is you'll have plenty of time for boys. But let a good church boy find you."

I wasn't happy with his answers, but his soft smile and calm demeanor brought fresh air inside his red pickup truck.

"Let me know when you want me to time you racing."

"Okay," I said. "Thanks for the ride home, and for the conversation."

Once inside the house, I couldn't wait to show off my ribbons: one for the dash, and the other for the relay. "Where's everyone at?" I asked.

Mike, Edward, and Thomas came from the bedroom. Mary and Joe were in the living room watching television. Mama came from our bedroom.

"How'd you do? Mama asked.

I hid my ribbons behind my back. Thomas tried to snatch them, but they were too tight in my hand.

"Our relay team came in first place. I ran the third leg. In the 100-yard dash, guess what? I came in. . ." I waited just like the officials at the race to shoot the gun.

"Oh, tell us," Mike said.

"I came in second place, behind one of my teammates."

"Congratulations!" Mama said.

Edward rustled my hair. "Good job."

Mike shoved my shoulders. "Maybe one day you'll be able to beat me." He smiled.

"Why do you kids have to make everything competitive?" Mama asked. "Maggie, there's some dinner for you still warm in the oven."

Mary sat at the dinner table with me while I ate. Joe went back into the living room to watch the television. Mike and Thomas prepared our lunches, talking back and forth between each other like I couldn't hear them.

Edward came from the bathroom. He patted my back and walked into the kitchen to help with the lunches. "Don't listen to those two."

"Maggie, don't forget to lay out your school clothes," Mama hollered from the front of the house. "I've gathered Mary's."

Mike and my brothers had finished preparing the lunches. I told Joe to turn off the TV. I turned the kitchen and dining room lights off. Mary and I tapped each other in play until we reached the bedroom.

I sorted through what I wanted to wear tomorrow, thinking about what Uncle Ted had said: I was a church girl, too young for a boyfriend, and a boy should approach me, not the reverse.

The only problem was that I had already slipped my note inside Raymond's locker, but signing it with an 'M' meant he wouldn't know the note came from me. I decided maybe I should follow Uncle Ted's suggestion.

. . . .

Mr. Hucklebee, our bus driver, honked the horn.

The school bus stopped abruptly. A car had darted in front of the bus before he could turn into the high school's driveway.

It was Susan in their shiny, red convertible. She loved for everyone to see her in it. This morning wasn't any different.

The bus stopped in front of the school. The principal greeted us. "Is anyone hurt? I had just parked when I saw Susan's mother pull in front of the bus."

"No," Mr. Hucklebee said, "but, you need to talk to her mother."

"I will."

Cheryl, Sarah, and Jackie were sitting next to the flower

bed at the school entrance. I didn't want to talk to them about Raymond not being at the track meet. I know they would ask. I waited to be the last one off of the bus.

"Hi girls." I mustered up a happy face. "Let's hurry and get to the bathroom before Susan and the others crowd it."

"Wait a minute," Cheryl said. "Did you see those idiots?"

Although I knew exactly what she meant, I didn't want to give time for them to ask me about Raymond and the track meet. So, I answered. "What do you mean?"

Jackie, Sarah, and Cheryl walked fast to keep up with me. "You know," Cheryl said, "Susan's mother speeding, cutting the bus off? I bet she was late for work again."

"Oh yeah," I said. "I saw that. Her mother will probably get a warning for driving fast while buses are unloading. They're on the school board."

When we turned the corner for the bathroom, Susan walked inside. We stopped.

"Let's go to our lockers instead."

We walked down the crowded hallway to the junior high section of the school. I tried talking about everything, but the track meet. The look on the girls faces told me they knew something wasn't right.

"Wait a minute, Maggie," Sarah said. "You're stalling. Was he there or not?"

"The relay team came in first place, and I came in second for the 100-"

"What about Raymond?" Sarah asked again. "You're stalling. Was he there or not?"

I hesitated before answering. Then someone bumped into me.

"Hello, Maggie."

I turned around. It was Raymond. He had his usual good cologne. He smiled with quotation marks on each side of his lips.

"I was at the track meet yesterday. Boy, you can run fast."

Why couldn't I open my mouth instead of standing there like a child? That's when I felt a nudge.

"Thank you," I said. "Where were you sitting?"

"I stood against the bleachers. When's your next meet?"

"Next week Wednesday in Newaygo. Will you be there?"

"Don't know. I'll try. Well, I have to get to class."

"He *was* there," I whispered to myself.

At my next two meets, I didn't see Raymond. I just saw

him in the hall. He'd wave sometimes. Saddened and disappointed, I thought *Why didn't I put my name on the note? Damn it. Sorry for the cuss word, God.*

Dear Diary,

My friends cornered me today in the girls' bathroom, asking questions about Raymond that I didn't have answers for. I really don't know if I want to talk about it to my friends.

Chapter 33

First Love?

Every day, Raymond would walk past my locker in the crowded halls, waving, with his quotation mark smile: a crooked, closed lip smile. I watched him walk with another girl. My heart hurt.

Cheryl bumped into me. "Stop staring at that boy."

"Yeah," Jackie said. "Since running on the track team, your popularity is greater than ever. There many boys in the junior high would like to be your boyfriend, if they can pass your brothers."

"But he's my first love." I held my books against my chest.

"How can he be your first love when he doesn't even know you like him?" Sarah asked. "Focus on your track meet."

I smirked. "You're right, but he's still my first love."

We did our secret wave and walked away to our next classes: Cheryl and I to math, Sarah to english and Jackie to science.

When I got home from school, I went to the living room.

The television was turned on until we finished our homework. The only choice the twins had was to color inside their coloring books.

"Maggie," Mama called. "Help me set the dinner table."

I dragged my feet along the floor, setting each plate on the table, and then the silverware.

"Why are you so sad, Maggie?" Mama asked.

"No reason."

"There must be something."

"Can I talk about it later?"

We sat at the table with the rest of the family. Mike shared about today's event that happened to him. Edward and Thomas didn't say anything.

"What about you, Maggie?" Mama asked.

The family had been talking about track. My aunts, brothers, and sister would begin to attend the track meets. Since Uncle Ted and Uncle John worked in town, they'd come after work, if they could.

There was a track meet tomorrow in a certain town and, because of my color, there were times I began to grow more concerned and scared.

"Mama?" I twirled my spoon in my potatoes then dropped

it onto my plate. "I'm scared to run my best."

"Maggie," Mama said. "You can't be telling me the truth. The entire family will be there to support you."

"But what if one of the girls trips me or calls me a nigger?"

Their eyes stared at me in disbelief. Even the twins. They dropped their silverware on their plates. Their almost empty glasses Kool-Aid thumped on the table. Then silence.

"What do you mean?" Mama asked. "You might not be able to stop the name calling, but you can defeat them by running your best."

"But Mama-"

"No buts," Mama said. "I hope I've raised you kids to fight diversity with winning, not being scared." She exhaled. "Now, you will run that race, and you will beat all of them. We'll be sitting on the top bleacher cheering and yelling." Mama sat back in her seat and held my hand. "You will win."

"Raise your hands if you will be there to support Maggie," Mike said.

Thomas, Edward, and Mama raised their hands. When I looked at Mary and Joe, they slowly raised their hands.

"We're scared for you, Maggie," Mary said.

"With the family there, I'll be just fine."

"Then we'll be there," Joe said.

I glanced at everyone around the table holding their hands high in the air.

"Tomorrow, I'll run with no fear."

. . . .

Wednesday morning, 6:00, and it's dark outside. Mama didn't have to wake me this morning. I slid from underneath the covers, careful not to wake Mary.

"You're up early," Mama whispered as she pulled our bedroom curtain aside. "Excited about today?"

"Yeah. I can't stop thinking about it." I fumbled through the closet, changing my mind about what to wear.

"Remember, the entire family will be there to cheer you on."

After breakfast, it was my turn to watch for the bus. Mary watched with me.

"The bus is coming down by Ole Man Harris' house," Mary said.

Her voice was soft, so I helped and hollered a second time

to make sure my brothers heard me. Edward was always late. Mama walked to the bathroom to hurry him along.

The bus squealed as it stopped in front of our house. Edward, the last one on, rushed before Mr. Williams closed the doors.

Mama waved.

I sat in my same seat, but near the aisle. Mary sat next to the window. She and I waved back to Mama.

On the way to school, I thought about dinner last night and my family's support to run this afternoon with no fear.

I remembered standing at the piano and looking up at the pictures of Jesus Christ first and then Dr. Martin Luther King.

Our family prayed every night before bed. If Mama was home before we got on the school bus, we'd pray for a blessed day.

This morning when we stood in front of the Jesus Christ wooden picture, I prayed for strength. Then I looked at Dr. Martin Luther King. "Dr. King, I hear you march for freedom and courage. Today, I want to run with the same courage you have for all Americans, but, most importantly, for the colored race."

Cheryl, Sarah, Jackie, and I walked into school. If we wanted to use the bathroom, there was no getting around the shared junior high and high school bathroom. Earlier in the school year, the girls had jammed me and my friends inside the bathroom stalls and crowded the mirror, but no longer. Being popular had it's perks. People spoke to me when I walked down the hall. My friends and I weren't shoved into the stalls.

Despite my popularity, Susan and her friends still never spoke to me and snubbed their noses when I walked pass them. In gym class, Susan and her friends would close the door in me and Cheryl's faces, snicker, and point their fingers at us.

Today, the day of the race, when Cheryl and I walked into the locker room, Mrs. Pollock tapped on the window and pointed for us to come see her.

"Maggie and Cheryl," Mrs. Pollock said, "have the two of you been showering?"

I looked at Cheryl, stunned. We answered, "Yes, Mrs. Pollock. All week."

She looked out the window at Susan and tapped her forehead with the eraser tip of her pencil. "I'll take care of this," she said. "You two had better get dressed before you're late."

While dressing, I silently thanked the Lord for helping us with gym. It wasn't on my prayer list.

As the day went on, I'd see Raymond between classes. Although my friends told me to forget about him, it was hard to move on.

Cheryl tapped me on my shoulder. "You need to be focusing on the race this afternoon and not him."

I sighed. "You're right."

"There is only one hour left before you have to get ready," she said. "Get your head together. It's a beautiful day, and everybody will be there to see you cross that finish line."

Mrs. Pollock interrupted us. "Maggie, your teacher gave you permission to leave class early. I'm holding a meeting in the gym with the entire girls' team. Please meet us there in five minutes."

I closed my locker. Cheryl had a curious look on her face. "I'll see you at the meet, Cheryl," I said. "Let me know what I missed in class."

When I reached the gym, a few girls sat on the bleachers. They seemed calm and relaxed. My stomach was in knots as I became more nervous.

The meeting lasted ten minutes. Mrs. Pollock dismissed us to the locker room to change into out track uniforms, but not before reminding us of a few more things.

"Don't forget to bring your school clothes and homework," she said. "Remember Principal Jackson will ride with us on the bus."

We walked to the bus. Horns honked. Before I stepped onto the bus, I looked back and saw cars lined up. Some of the parents had decided to follow us.

Mama's station wagon was the third car back. Mary and Joe sat in the front. They leaned out the window, called my name, and waved frantically. "Good luck!" They called.

My foot was on the bottom step of the bus when Mike and Edward hollered and leaned outside the car. "Mama said to tell you that the rest of the family will meet us there." They had silly grins on their faces. "Run your butt off, sis."

"I will!"

The bus ride took thirty minutes. When we arrived, the bleachers were half-full. The driver parked underneath the trees for shade, along with Mama and the other families.

Mrs. Pollock stood up in the middle aisle of the bus. "Everyone should stretch. The track meet will begin immediately after the national anthem. Field events first."

Once the team had departed the bus, Mrs. Pollock and Principal Jackson held me back. "We got word that some of the kids might not be kind to you on the track," Principal Jackson said.

"Please stay close to me or the team," Mrs. Pollock said. "Don't wander off."

I paused at the bottom step. I almost didn't want to run, but my entire family would be in the grandstands. I stepped off the bus behind Mrs. Pollock and Principal Jackson.

"You run your tail off, young lady," the bus driver said. He had driven the bus to most of the Wednesday track meets but never said much. Today was different. Maybe it was because he had heard the rumors.

"I will," I said.

Our team stretched in the shade. Mrs. Pollock stood nearby with Principal Jackson. Other principals were in attendance and came to shake his hand. They all looked around the field and then at me, although I wasn't the only colored girl running today.

"Remember to stay near us," Mrs. Pollock whispered. "The other colored girls were given the same warning by their coaches too."

Our team made it to the finals in the 4x4 relay. As

Mrs. Pollock instructed, we stayed near the shade until an announcement came from the intercom. "All participants running in the 4x4 relay final, please report to the starting line."

Gail walked me to my spot. "Don't worry, Maggie. Stay calm, be patient, and wait until I hand you the baton." Gail was half way to her spot when she turned around. She cupped two hands around her mouth and yelled, "Run that, anchor!"

There were four fast runners on our relay team. I wasn't worried about that race. All season, our team had beaten everyone. A runner would have to be close to bump me out of my lane. I was worried about the 100-yard dash.

The officials stood next to each lane of the relay to make sure all baton exchanges were correct. The gun fired.

Gail was our third leg. Another runner began to close in on her. "Stick. Stick," Gail said to me. I grabbed the baton and ran. The crowd roared and jumped up and down. I crossed the finish line into the arms of the team, happy.

The official made an announcement. "Half hour before the 100-yard dash."

I had expected to have more time between events. "Mrs. Pollock," I said still out of breath from my race. "I just ran the 4x4 relay finals."

"You'll be fine," she said. "Keep warming up."

White girls walked by staring, crossing their eyes. Some pointed in my direction. "Look at that nigger," one girl said. "Look at all the niggers," another said.

"Stay focused, Maggie," Gail said. "When you run the 100-yard dash leave them in your dust."

I continued to warm up.

"Anyone running in the first heat of the 100-yard dash, please report," the announcer said.

Immediately after the first heat, the officials asked the second and last heat runners to line up.

"Remember, Maggie," Mrs. Pollock said, "runners with the best times will make it to the preliminaries, and then the finals."

When the gun shot, I expected girls to shove or push me out of my lane. They didn't. I won with no confrontation.

My team crowded around me, smiling. When I looked up into the bleachers, my family stood and clapped their hands.

"Mrs. Pollock, what happened?"

"You won! That's what happened."

"But no one bothered me."

Fifteen minutes later, the official announced with a louder voice, "All participants running in the preliminary 100-yard dash, please report to the starting line."

"Remember what we talked about, Maggie," Mrs. Pollock said.

I looked around in the grandstands. My family sat next to each other, except for Mike, Edward, and Thomas. They leaned on the fence that went around the track.

Mrs. Pollock appeared more nervous than me, which I didn't understand. I had won the first race with no problems. She pushed her hair from her face numerous times and kept patting me on my shoulders.

"I'll be all right," I said. "My family is here. I've prayed and pointed to the sky."

The runners stood in their lanes. This time, I was in the lane closest to the inside of the field. Another colored girl was in the middle.

"On your mark." A pause. "Get set." A longer pause. Then the gun shot.

The heat started with everyone running together. By the middle of the 100, two of us began to pull ahead. The other colored girl lagged behind.

"Run, Maggie!" Mike, Thomas, and Edward yelled, waving their arms.

I couldn't get my legs to move any faster. I came in second.

I crouched over, my hands on my knees. My brothers' voices were in the distance but grew closer.

"Maggie, are you all right?" Mike asked.

Mrs. Pollock hugged me. The rest of the team consoled me. This was only the third time I hadn't come in first place.

I looked for Mama and the rest of my family. Mike, Thomas, and Edward had run to the finish line and held onto the top of the fence.

"You have to pull away from the pack," Mike said.

"Yeah," Edward said.

I tried to catch my breath. "My legs wouldn't move any faster."

Raymond stood up from his seat on the bleacher with a concerned look on his face. He pointed to the start line and moved his arm toward the finish line. "Win!" He shouted.

"The final heat of the 100-yard dash will start in 15 minutes," the announcer said.

Mrs. Pollock jerked her head in disbelief.

"What's wrong, Mrs. Pollock?" I asked.

"I'll be right back." She hurried toward the organizer of the tournament.

"The start time is too soon for the 100-yard dash final," Gail explained to me. "Last year, there was 45 minutes in between."

Shortly after Mrs. Pollock and the principal walked away, the runner who thought she was unbeatable, Megan Hunsley, stood in front of me. My team gathered around me, showing support.

Megan crossed her arms. Some of her team was with her. "You better lose this race," she said.

"And if I don't?" I inched away from my team and crossed my arms.

"You're gonna try and win?" Megan's lips twisted. "Maybe-"

"Maggie?" Mrs. Pollock walked back to our team, Principal Jackson beside her.

Megan noticed Mrs. Pollock and walked away, expecting her team to follow her.

"What did she say?" Mrs. Pollock asked.

"Nothing much."

"Maggie, you'll have to warm up now: a slow walk and stretches. There's nothing I can do about the wait time."

Shortly before the 100-yard dash final, the team circled around me, giving pointers. Then they escorted me to the start line.

"On your mark." Pause. "Get set." Mama and the rest of the family made eye contact with me. Uncle Ted and Uncle John walked through the gate. All the coloreds in the stands stood up. The gun shot.

I started out faster than in the preliminaries. The runner in the next lane bumped into me, but I kept my concentration. During the middle of the race, someone else bumped me, causing me to stumble, but I stayed in my lane. . . barely. If I crossed outside the white lines on either side of my lane, I'd be disqualified. I gathered my composure, focused on the race, and, said a prayer that Mama always said to us: "The Lord is my shepherd." The finish line was in sight, and I was behind. Then I crossed the finish line and fell to the ground.

"Nigger!" someone hollered.

I looked around but didn't see the person. All the coloreds, even the coloreds who had lost their races, cheered. My team gathered around me.

Megan had lost to me. When I looked at her, she frowned.

"I'll get you next time, nigger," she mouthed.

"But, not this time."

. . . .

The school bus door opened. I was the last one off.

"I heard you ran a heck of a race yesterday." Mr. Hucklebee smiled. The most he'd said to me all year was "Sit down" or "Stop yelling out the window."

"Thank you, Mr. Hucklebee."

"If I'm here next year, maybe I'll get a chance to see you run again."

I stepped away from the bus, stunned by the people standing in front of the school. Cheryl, Sarah, and Jackie stood in front of our normal spot by the school light post, surrounded by kids from the junior high and some from the high school.

The junior high track team, Mrs. Pollock, and Principal Jackson were waiting for my bus to arrive.

Our track team had come in first place for the first time. The school clapped, cheered, and hollered our names.

"Okay, everyone," the principal said. "It's time to begin the school day."

"Seems like principal would call everyone to the gym," I said to Mrs. Pollock.

"He wanted to do something different," she said. "And this is different. It's a beautiful day. The sun is out. Just enjoy it."

Everyone wanted to see our ribbons.

I stood at my locker with Cheryl and Sarah. Someone tapped my shoulder.

"What's wrong?" I asked.

Cheryl crossed her eyes.

"What?"

"Congratulations." Raymond was behind me, smelling good, as usual, and smiling.

"Uh, um."

Sarah nudged my shoulder.

"I mean, thank you." I stared into his eyes. "You were at the meet. You stood on the top bleecher."

"Yeah. You sure can run fast."

I remembered that Mama always said to be humble. "I guess so," I said.

The last bell rung. The hallway emptied quickly.

· · · ·

If it wasn't for the track team, I'd still be plain ole Maggie, the third oldest child after Mike and Edward, and one of the six Hammond kids.

No matter how fast I ran around the track, it looked like Raymond Grant would never let me win over his heart as my first love. My shyness and religion stopped me. I settled for his brief wave and quotation mark smile. Occasionally, his friends and mine shared a lunch table.

Mama had reminded my brothers, sister, and I to come home right after school on our last day. We tossed our bags on the dining room table, this time without our school books. This was a ritual.

Mary and Joe had completed second grade. Mary had grown taller than Joe but was skinny. Mama walked into the house as we changed into our everyday clothes.

"How was everyone's last day of school? I mean, half day of school?"

The boys hollered from their bedroom, "Good."

I mumbled, "Mine was good too."

"Let me change out of these hospital clothes. We can sit

around the dining room table."

"Mama, is it all right if my friends come over this weekend?"

"I don't mind if they come on Saturday," she said, "after I get home from work."

I hurried from the table.

"Wait a minute," Mama said. "Where you goin'?"

"To call and let them know."

"Why don't you wait until after supper? The dishes need to be washed and the food put away."

"Okay."

• • • •

It was Saturday morning, two weeks after school let out. Sarah and her family were doing something, so we changed the date to meet at my house.

We were older now and didn't play hopscotch or jump rope. Instead, we used sticks to design a big tic-tac-toe game on the ground near the tree between Uncle Ted's house and my house.

"Has your family decided what you're gonna do this summer?" I asked Sarah.

"Daddy said the entire family will visit his brother and sisters at a family reunion. After that, we'll visit Mama's grandmother. She's not doin' so well."

Cheryl, Jackie, and I looked at each other. "I'm sorry," we said.

"I hope she feels better," I said.

Sarah gave me a hug and then, changed the subject. "What about you guys?" she asked.

"Well," Cheryl said, "I'm visiting my cousin down south for part of the summer. We will be back home near the end of summer."

"I don't know yet," Jackie said. "Daddy and Mama haven't made up their minds."

"And you, Maggie?" my friends asked.

I kicked the dirt, my head down. "The usual: picking onions or cherries," I mumbled.

"But your mama works more hours, I thought," Sarah said.

My friends and I looked at her.

"I wasn't trying to be mean or anything," Sarah said. "I feel bad that we get to go on a vacation and you and your family pick crops all summer long."

"I know you didn't mean it in a hurtful way," I said to her. "She only works a few hours at the nursing facility in Fremont. It's still not enough money."

After a half hour we got bored playing with our oversized tic-tac-toe game. We raced and then walked up the road.

"Will you guys miss junior high?" Sarah asked.

"I don't have anything to talk about, except for Maggie running after Raymond." Cheryl said.

"Summer has just started, and I don't want to think about junior high right now."

"You don't have any memorable moments?" Jackie asked Cheryl.

"And what are your memories?" Cheryl asked Jackie.

Jackie thought for a moment before answering. "A moment for me, too, was watching Maggie run after Raymond."

"What about you, Sarah?" I asked.

"Let me see," she said. "I think a memorable moment for me was when you never backed down from Susan. For three years, she harassed you, and every time, you stood up to her. I was proud."

"What about you, Maggie?" Cheryl asked.

"Most certainly, wanting Raymond to be my boyfriend, and the steps I took to try and make that happen, only to be heartbroken."

"Anything else?"

"What about Susan," Sarah asked.

"No," I said. "There will always be Susans in the world. Racism is everywhere."

Cheryl said, "Let's put our arms around each other."

We did what Cheryl asked. She put her arm around me. I put my arm around Sarah, and Sarah put her arm around Jackie.

"See?" Cheryl said. "The four of us became friends in elementary school and have remained friends all the way through junior high, learning and growing. Those are our memories."

Dear Diary,

Today was the last day of junior high and **another** *new start on my life.*